CURSES & SACRIFICES

Book 12 of
THE WARDEN

FELICIA JEDLICKA

*I dedicate this book to Whitney, whom I frustrate endlessly
with my cliffhangers.
Hang in there, girl—I'm not done yet!*

SISTER WITCHES
THE DEVIL'S SHADOW
THE DEVIL'S SOUL

DESTINY REJECTED
DESTINY RECLAIMED
DESTINY RAZED
DESTINY RESTORED

DÉJÀ VU

SAVE THE HUMANS

THE NECROMANCER'S CHILD

<u>**THE NEBRASKA APOCALYPSE NOVELS**</u>
CORN COWS AND THE APOCALYPSE
COW TIPPING AFTER THE APOCALYPSE
CORN HUSKING AFTER THE APOCALYPSE

<u>**THE WARDEN SERIES**</u>
SUCCESSORS
RIVALS
LOVERS AND LIARS
BAD BLOOD
TENANTS AND TYRANTS
THE RING BEARER
GODS AND MONSTERS
BEASTS AND BURDENS
MAGIC AND MAYHEM
FORK IN THE ROAD
DETAILS AND DEADLINES
*CURSES AND SACRIFICES**
*WITCHES AND WOLVES**
*SAINTS AND SERPENTS**
*ENEMIES AND ALLIES**

*MARRIED TO DEATH**

Curses & Sacrifices

Felicia Jedlicka

1

GYPSY BREATHED A SIGH of relief as the skid hit the rooftop. She put the brake in place and shut down the helicopter's engine. It had been a long trip, and even with her uploaded flying lessons, she wasn't comfortable with the variable weather conditions this far north. As if gale-force winds weren't enough to tighten her grip on the cyclic, there was always the occasional glass-shattering blast wave to worry about... or dragons.

Gypsy unstrapped herself and peered out the windshield at her arriving escort. Despite the early hours, the prison's security was on point. The lookouts had no doubt called in their impromptu guests the minute they caught sight of the helicopter over the dark horizon.

Gypsy climbed out of the cabin and approached her favorite spark plug. She was legitimately pleased to engage with Efrat again, but she was a little disappointed not to see her favorite Texan by his side. His particular charm was growing on her. She was certain he didn't reciprocate that sentiment, but time was usually a better predictor for her friendships than first impressions.

Efrat brought his arms forward and away from his sides—the equivalent of cocking a gun in his case. She bit her lip, trying not to mock him with an unrestrained grin. Nevertheless, she raised her hands to reveal her empty palms, surrendering to his authority. She knew he was dangerous—more dangerous than anyone gave him credit for, but much like Daniel McGrath, she could see a reluctance in his armament. He had no desire to hurt her. Not yet anyway.

"Since when did the roof become our official landing pad?" Efrat called to her over the slowing whir of the chopper's blades.

Gypsy shrugged and glanced back at her newly acquired bird. It cost a pretty penny, but it hadn't come out of her account, so she didn't have to worry about it. "I'm afraid my employer doesn't understand the meaning of the phrase no-fly zone. And he hates traveling by land. Too slow."

"Your employer sounds like a douchebag."

Gypsy tipped her head and perked her brow. He wasn't wrong. Her employment had been more than satisfactory on the money front, and there were certainly perks to having such a powerful man in her corner, but his personality required a degree of tolerance... and coddling. "Where's your other half? I was looking forward to being greeted with some down-home Southern charm."

Efrat frowned and averted his eyes to the ground. "He's inside the Medusa statue."

"Oh." Gypsy wasn't sure what that meant, but by the look on Efrat's face, it wasn't good. "Can't get him out, I take it?" Efrat shook his head despondently, jaw tight as if he were fighting back more emotions than he preferred to reveal to her. "Rough week then?"

Efrat glared at her, but she held back any sign of amusement so he knew she wasn't mocking his distress. She wasn't unfamiliar with the loss of a colleague, and she considered it one of the more underrated griefs that people had to endure. Recognizing her sincerity in the statement, he scoffed and nodded. "You have no idea."

"I'm sorry. I know you and Tex were friends."

"Duke," Efrat corrected a little defensively. Never mind that the man's given name was Duane, his nickname was as much a part of his identity as his southern accent. Or at least it had been.

Gypsy could feel the moment getting heavy. If they continued on this path, there was bound to be hugging or tears—and there was no need to embarrass the man like that. "How about I kick these two douchebags out of my chopper and we can fly off to Tijuana together?"

Efrat looked back at the chopper. His frown softened, and his lip tipped up a little. "I'd love to, but knowing my luck, I would short out the engine and we would crash and burn before we made it to the equator." Efrat showed off his dazzling blue hands.

Gypsy shrugged. "Well, it would be a hot ride either way."

Efrat's brow dipped at her semi-flirtatious morbidness. "You really are a strange cat, you know that, right?"

"Strange as they come." Gypsy shifted to see who had come through the roof exit. She met eyes with Cori. Dressed in a black coat two sizes too big, and her hair blowing in her face, Gypsy still recognized her instantly. "Ah, crap," Gypsy mumbled. She had expected to have an altercation with the woman. Cutting off her hand was bound to have some lasting consequences for their already turbulent relationship. However, she had hoped to make it off the roof before the fisticuffs began. It was too damn cold up here, and the lighting was shit. "I don't suppose an apology will get me out of this fight."

Efrat glanced back at Cori's approach and stiffened his back upright into a proper little soldier. Whatever levity Gypsy had developed in the conversation had instantly evaporated. "I don't think so," Efrat said quietly. "She's having a worse week."

Gypsy wondered what was worse than losing one of their own, but she didn't have time to inquire.

Cori moved toward her; eyes bright with venom that increased with each step. She could see there was no chance of making peace with the woman now. At best, she could have a proper row with her and exhaust the anger out of her once and for all.

Cori stopped beside Efrat and looked her over. Gypsy recognized the attempt to search her for weapons, but the woman was not skilled enough to identify anything beyond the bulge of a gun holster. Not that it mattered since, like the last time she visited, Gypsy was under strict orders not to harm "the good guys," unless absolutely necessary. The fact that cutting off Cori's hand became necessary last time was not her fault. Strictly speaking, it was Cori's fault. The woman's doggedness had been extremely inconvenient to her rescue efforts.

"What the hell are you doing here?" Cori asked, not bothering to hide even a sliver of her contempt.

Gypsy was relieved that she hadn't outright attacked her, but that didn't mean Cori wasn't poised for any excuse to start a fight. Gypsy needed to be very careful about what she said so she wouldn't set the woman off.

"I've come for the other hand," Gypsy announced with a wicked smile.

"You bitch!" Cori only hesitated a second before pulling her gun.

"Cori, no!" Efrat grabbed her wrist just before the pistol let out a resounding crack.

Gypsy belatedly jumped out of the bullet's original path—legitimately fearing for her life. She was disappointed that she had underestimated the woman's level of anger. Not to mention her willingness to *actually* kill her. Cori had always been unpredictable, no doubt, but she wasn't usually so lethal. Perhaps Duke's loss was harder on her than Gypsy would have estimated. She wasn't aware of any romantic relationship between them, but perhaps Cori's home life wasn't as June and Ward as it appeared from the outside.

"Cori, stop!" Efrat struggled with her, using a few snaps of electricity to get her to release her grip on the gun. It *thunked* onto the tar roof, and Efrat kicked it away from her.

"Let go of me!" she screamed at Efrat. "You're hurting me!" He immediately released his painful grip on her wrists and retracted from her. They exchanged a look that Gypsy didn't quite understand—guilt. She understood Efrat's guilt, but what did Cori have to feel guilty about?

Cori rubbed her wrists and turned her attention back to Gypsy. "If you come near me again, I will kill you!" As serious as the situation was, Gypsy still couldn't resist puffing her lips into a mocking kiss. Cori darted forward, but Efrat jumped ahead of her, holding her back with the broad side of his arm so he wouldn't electrocute her. "Do you understand me, you psychopathic bitch?" Cori's voice nearly broke with the force of her words.

Gypsy straightened up, shifting her shoulders back and raising her chin. She didn't mind being called names—she rather enjoyed her long-standing title of bitch, but for some reason, she didn't like it when Cori said it. It probably had to do with the fact that Cori hadn't earned the right to call her that yet. Discounting a stray timeline in which Gypsy killed everyone Cori loves, she had done virtually nothing to the woman—besides irritating her. In the back of her mind, Gypsy could hear a little voice demanding that she show Cori just how psychopathic she could be, but fortunately, there was a much louder voice telling her to do her duty.

"I do understand," Gypsy said in an almost respectful tone. "But I'm not going anywhere, so you need to redefine your definition of *near* while we work together."

Cori ceased struggling against Efrat's restraint. "What are you talking about?"

"I have a job to do, and your opinion of me takes no precedence over my duties."

"What job?" Cori narrowed her eyes.

"Bonjour, Cori." A pair of long legs, punctuated by high heels, scissored their way around the back of the chopper. Leona ducked beneath the tail, dragging a tiny wheeled suitcase with her.

Cori's anger seemed to dim as she stared at the woman's shimmering purple lips, heavy eyeliner, and layered brown locks. The fem-wolf's skirt was short as it tended to be, but to add to her mystique, her shirt was completely sheer. Her bandeau bra was barely enough to contain her, but that didn't much matter when she had no shame for what was underneath. Even after two kids, the woman had maintained a figure that both men and women yearned for.

Gypsy noted that Efrat had taken a particular interest in her physique, dragging his eyes down her legs and back up to her exposed bust line. He obviously didn't get much exposure to women, certainly not any as alluring as this. Since he had never shown any interest in Gypsy's overt sexuality, she presumed the elemental preferred *girly* women. Little did he know Leona didn't fall into that category any more than Gypsy. Even so, she was nice to look at—when she wasn't talking.

"It's been a long time," Leona purred in her dulcet French accent.

Cori's mouth dropped open, but nothing came out. Gypsy had heard Leona brag on more than one occasion about her hold over the woman, but to see it up close was something of a disappointment. Just when Cori had impressed her with an attempted murder, her high ranking was slipping away with a werewolf girl crush.

"Not long enough." Cori finally communicated. She brushed away Efrat's grasp and squared her shoulders. "What are you doing here? Shouldn't you be held up in a cage somewhere, shaving the fur off your back?"

Gypsy snorted, trying to contain her laughter. Leona tossed a scathing glare in her direction, but she just shrugged it off. If Frederique didn't intimidate her, she certainly wouldn't be cowed by her sister.

"I'm here to discuss an alliance," Leona said.

"An alliance?" Cori perked a brow. "Don't tell me you're having another domestic dispute with an ex."

"No, this is a far less personal issue, but nonetheless, one of the utmost importance. One which I will speak to Danato about immediately."

"You know I didn't have you down on the schedule. Maybe you should come back another time. Gypsy, why don't you and your bitch fly back to hell? I'll pencil you both in for: over my dead body."

"That can be arranged." Leona took a threatening step forward.

"Speaking of dead bodies," Efrat interjected, stepping in front of Cori. "You will need to back the fuck off."

"And just who are you?" Leona looked him over with condescending amusement.

"I'm *her* bitch." Efrat nodded to Cori. Gypsy chortled at the joke, drawing a few glances.

"Is that so?" Leona took another step forward, but this time she disguised it as a seductive approach. She pushed in close, putting her breasts against Efrat's chest. To his credit, the elemental didn't look the least bit flustered by her sexual intimidation. "Maybe I should introduce myself?"

"Maybe you should," Efrat taunted her.

Gypsy groaned and took a step back, then forward. She rubbed her head, trying to ease the pressure building in her leashed brain. Everyone looked at her odd display, but she couldn't help it. The words she didn't want to say were fighting to get out of her lips, and the words she wanted to say were getting caught in her throat. She hated this part of her job. The part that kept her behavior within "reasonable" parameters and forcefully balanced her morality when her lacking conscience did not.

"Something you wish to say, Grace?"

Gypsy tried to shake her head, but even that was beyond her scope of responses, which was too bad. She wanted to see this fight. She wanted nothing more than to watch Efrat knock the fem-wolf down a peg just as he had Callin, but her instructions were to protect Leona if necessary. And a threat from an elemental definitely qualified as "if necessary."

"Yes," the word slipped between her clenched teeth.

"Go on, Grace. What aren't you telling me?"

"You need to back off." Gypsy finally gave in and released the words. "Efrat is not just another lackey guard."

"Then who is he?" Leona's eyes trailed down his fit body, trying to determine how this mere human might force Gypsy into a protective mode.

"He's Frankenstein's monster with an emphasis on the '*spark of being*.'" Leona looked at her baffled. "He's the elemental."

Leona's mood changed instantly from pomposity to a childlike delight. "Really?" She looked Efrat over again, this time pausing on his slightly shimmering hands. "You're the electrical one, aren't you?"

"That's me—lightning in a bottle."

"I've heard so much about you. I've looked forward to our meeting. I'm told that your power is quite unparalleled. Even against werewolves." Leona reached out, trailing her finger down Efrat's arm until it reached his hand. The slight shock that transferred between them wasn't enough to repel the handshake she bestowed on him. Efrat looked more than uncomfortable by the contact and seemed to concentrate very hard on not electrocuting her. When Leona finally released him, she was panting with exhilaration. Efrat glanced at Gypsy—no doubt searching for the answers.

"You're gonna be very popular among the fem-wolves," Gypsy whispered and gave him a wink.

"Great," Efrat mumbled and took a step away from Leona. Since Cori chose that moment to come forward, it almost looked as if the elemental was seeking refuge behind her.

"If you're done going through heat, Leona, maybe we can go over the reason for your unannounced visit," Cori griped.

"This is an interesting pairing." Leona waved her finger between the two of them. "Didn't this man try to kill you once?"

"Twice," Gypsy reported, eliciting glares from Cori and Efrat. "Don't worry about it, Leona. Everybody tries to kill Cori, eventually." Gypsy locked eyes with Cori so she could watch her rage come to a steady simmer. "But she's much too clever to be killed." Dubious of the compliment, Cori's anger turned to confusion. "As you well know, Leona." This time it was the fem-wolf's turn to throw eye daggers at her. "Better to keep her on your good side, I think." And finally, it was Gypsy's turn to glower. Though Leona was far from intimidated by her, there was an unnatural coldness in her gaze that made even the bravest soul shudder.

"Oui, I was just thinking that." Leona moved to stand before Cori. "Still, it must be strange for you," she spoke with sincerity, "being surrounded by your former mortal enemies."

Before Cori could attempt to respond, a snap of electricity forced everyone's attention back to Efrat. He didn't move, but the static in the air had increased substantially, raising the hair on both women.

Leona's smile returned, and she took a deep breath. She moved back to Efrat. "It's good we are all friends now." She leaned in and kissed both of Efrat's cheeks—leaving perfect lip prints on each side.

"You have no right to come here unannounced, Leona," Cori said.

Leona closed her eyes and whispered something in French. "As a matter of fact, we were invited. Or didn't Renee tell you the top-floor renter would arrive after the renovations were complete?"

"No." Cori shook her head, but she was not answering Leona's question. "There is no way the board would let a fem-wolf rent the top floor."

"Oh, it's not me." Leona smiled. "I just came with him because we have mutual interests to discuss."

"Came with whom?" Cori glanced at the chopper, but since the back windows were tinted to near black, there was no way to see who the third guest was.

"Your renter." Leona stepped to one side just as the door to the helicopter's passenger hold opened. A long leg stepped down to the tarred roof, followed by the second. A tight-fitting suit jacket, a dark blue undershirt, and a thin black tie joined the emerging black slacks. The long black tresses, formerly begging to be placed in a ponytail, were cut off.

Besides his deathly pale skin, the only unchanged feature on him was his sparkling eyes. They belied the danger that lurked in the recesses of his mind—where an endless vacuum stored stolen memories. Each of them was a trophy to feed his ego and satisfy an almost vampiric lust for intellect and experience.

"Hello, Corinthia," Cleos said.

2

D ESPITE THE SMALL SMILE hiding on his stone-cold face, and the hunger stoking the glimmer in his gaze, Cori knew Cleos was not happy to see her. To say that they parted on bad terms was an understatement. Cleos had systematically tormented her until she hated him. Even though he saved her from the house entity's psychic invasion, she couldn't help but feel he was only doing it to keep a clear conscience, not because he actually cared for her.

Ever since she had accidentally invaded his mind, he had treated her like a leper. Denying their friendship had hurt her deeply. More deeply than she wanted to admit. Seeing him again brought it all back. The anger, bitterness, and feelings of abandonment that she knew any well-paid psychiatrist would classify as *daddy issues*.

Cleos straightened his tie and tugged down his suit jacket as he approached her. Efrat gave them a little space to talk but didn't go far. He most likely needed time to gauge Cori's mood before he could determine if this meeting was just unwelcome or potentially dangerous.

"It's good to see you." Cleos extended his hand to Cori. She looked down at the baited olive branch but didn't bite. He slowly lowered his hand, tugging on his cuffs as he did.

"What are you doing here, Cleos?" Cori took a step back.

"I'm your new tenant," he answered.

"Why? What are you planning to do here?"

"I plan to fix the massive cash flow problem this prison has. There's money in those artifacts Danato has been hoarding; we just have to figure out how to use them to get it."

"That should be exceptionally dangerous. Are these two your first guinea pigs?" Cori nodded to Gypsy and Leona.

"Oh, no, they aren't my underlings. They're my partners."

"Partners?" Cori looked between the two of them. "This is an odd entourage. My two least favorite people in the world."

"Leona turned out to be a fortuitous acquisition, but her sister was far more difficult to deal with, so she had to be dethroned. Gypsy, on the other hand..." Cleos reached over and pressed his hand against Gypsy's shoulder, dragging it down her arm before falling away. "Well, I sought her out."

"You sought her out?"

"Yes. I was certain that she would be an excellent asset in the battle ahead. I suppose I should thank you for introducing me to her." Cleos smirked and tapped his head.

Cori felt yet another little pang in her already raw heart. As if the last 24 hours hadn't ripped her to shreds already, Cleos was pouring vinegar in old and new wounds. It was too much. "You son of a bitch!" Cori lunged forward.

Efrat grabbed hold of her once more, dragging her back away from all of them. "Maybe we should postpone this meeting," he suggested.

"Efrat!" Ethan joined them on the roof with two guards trailing behind him. "What did I tell you about touching my wife?"

"What? This isn't—she..." Efrat babbled.

"Let her go," Ethan said as he passed by them.

Efrat scoffed and released her. Cori tried to finish what she had started, but Ethan held up his arm, stopping her in her tracks. She wasn't happy about the unspoken order, but she didn't want to undermine her husband's authority. Certainly not in front of these three.

"Cleos." Ethan threw out his hand.

"Ethan, don't," Cori warned, since it left Ethan open to his particular form of thievery. Ethan no doubt intended it as a peace offering, but since the mind reading also exposed much of Cori's life, it seemed like a violation more than a treaty.

Cleos looked over the offering with amusement. He even glanced back at Cori as he slipped his slender fingers inside Ethan's firm grip.

"Hello, Ethan." Cleos gave his hand a slight squeeze. "I wasn't expecting such a..." Cleos trailed off, his gaze drawing into a trance that Cori was all too familiar with. Cleos's eyes snapped back into real-time, and he stared at Ethan. "...warm greeting."

Their hands fell away, but they continued to stare at each other. "A lot has happened since you've been away," Ethan said.

"Yes, it appears so." Cleos frowned and looked Ethan over carefully. Cleos's attention moved to Cori. She shook her head and panted as his hateful eyes turned somber and sincere. Of all the things she hated him for, that was the worst. How dare he try to be nice to her now. "Cori," he breathed.

"Don't," she snapped. "It's no concern of yours. My life is nothing for you to be concerned about."

Cleos stared at her for a moment, a small amount of anger returning to his face. It was better than his sympathy. "I will do anything in my power to help," Cleos told Ethan. "I assume Belus is already researching the text."

"Yes, we've made copies and distributed them." Ethan's jaw clenched before he could speak again. "We need all the help we can get."

"Of course, as soon as I finish with Danato, I will look through it. I can do it faster." Cleos glanced over at Gypsy.

She perked her brow trying to glean what he wanted. "I'm sorry about... the other two, as well."

Ethan looked off in the distance and nodded. "Thank you."

"Once we get the child back, I'll begin studying the Medusa statue. Every problem has a solution. Even the ones set in stone."

Gypsy narrowed her eyes and looked at Cori for further information. Cori barely wanted Cleos to know the private details of her unraveling life, let alone Gypsy.

"I appreciate your help." Ethan turned his head slightly. "We both do." Cori glanced at Cleos again but didn't hold his gaze. Ethan looked at Gypsy and nodded at her. She gave him a civil nod back.

"Leona." Ethan nodded at Leona as well.

"Bonjour, Ethan," Leona said with a husky voice. Ethan looked away before she could bat her eyes and purse her lips at him.

"I'll go gather the bosses in the conference room. I don't think we'll all fit in Danato's office. My men can show you the way when you're ready."

"Thank you, Ethan," Cleos called after him, but he was looking at Cori. "I'm glad someone in this facility can stay focused under pressure."

Cori's anger reared up again, and she charged at Cleos. Efrat once again grabbed her, trying to subdue her.

"Efrat, what did I say?" Ethan called back to him.

"But she's—"

"Let her go!" Ethan yelled as he disappeared into the stairwell.

Efrat sighed and let her go. Cori rushed forward, but instead of tackling Cleos as she originally wanted to, she picked up her downed gun.

Gypsy jumped forward, prepared to defend Cleos, but he held up his hand, signaling that he didn't need her.

Cori came in fast, with her gun aimed, but stopped just shy of pushing it into his body. Cleos observed the gun aimed at his midsection and gave Cori his most notable simper. "Do you think you could really pull the trigger?"

"I wouldn't."

"You couldn't. Whether either of us likes it, we are intimately connected now. I doubt you could hurt me even if you wanted to."

"Let's try, anyway." Cori turned the butt of the gun upward and shoved it at Cleos's face. The weapon hit with a sickening smack, knocking him backward. He grabbed his mouth, touching his bleeding lip as he stared at Cori in shock.

"What the hell was that, Cori!" Cleos bellowed, losing every ounce of his sophisticated composure.

"Revenge."

"For what? Do you even remember why you are mad at me?"

"Remember? Do I remember you belittling me for an accident I had no control of? Do I remember how much of an ass you were?"

"Don't be overdramatic. I'm not the only one with a temper, Cori!"

"Don't put this on me. I wasn't the one who broke this." Cori motioned between them. "You were the one who pushed me away. If you expected me to be pining for your return, then you were sadly mistaken. I have long since given up on our friendship."

"No, you haven't," Cleos snarled.

"You can't speak for me anymore, Cleos. You don't know me." Cori lowered her gun and turned away.

"That's a lie!" Cleos licked the blood from his lip and took a step to go after her. Efrat moved forward, and Cleos regarded him with a measure of concern. "It's you who doesn't know me. It's you who underestimates me. You don't even know how dangerous I am. You never did."

Efrat's hands snapped with power, but Cleos didn't move away. "You think everything I did since that day was to hurt you. You think I pushed you away to break your little heart." Cori turned back to him, an icy indifference on her face. "Everything I have done since then—since the moment I met you...! Was for you!"

"Stop!" Cori flailed her hands out. "I don't have time for this. I don't have time to cater to your over-inflated ego."

Cleos sobered and nodded. "I know." He looked at Efrat, who was primed to electrocute him at any moment. He raised his hand and pressed it to his cheek. Efrat's electrical output increased to a threatening snap, but he still didn't attack.

Cleos gave his cheek a couple of fatherly pats before retracting. He leaned into Efrat's ear and whispered something to him before he moved away. Cleos offered his arm to Leona. "Ladies, shall we?"

Leona took his arm and allowed him to lead her off the roof. The two guards followed behind them, leaving Cori and Efrat to escort Gypsy.

"What did he say to you?" Cori asked Efrat.

Efrat frowned and looked after Cleos. "He said, 'You can thank me later.' What does that mean?"

"He probably dropped a memory bomb on you," Gypsy said.

"And just what the hell is that?" Efrat asked.

"It's usually a good thing. Once you get nice and cozy tonight for bed. You'll get a happy little bedtime story."

"Why would he give me a memory? I barely even know him?"

Gypsy shrugged. "Like I said, it's *usually* a good thing."

3

G YPSY COULDN'T HELP GLANCING at Cori from across the elevator. With her gun still perched against her shoulder, she was ready to aim at a moment's notice. However, she wasn't alert. She was in a daze. The extra glitter in her eyes, trying to claim the title of tears, bothered Gypsy. Actually, everything about the interactions on the roof bothered her. She warned Cleos that his little project was ill-timed, but now it seemed downright inappropriate. Whatever they had walked in on was too delicate for guns and heavy swearing. Emotionally infused environments were not Gypsy's strong suit, since it meant she would have to play nice.

She wasn't good at *nice*.

"What's going on?" she finally asked.

"What?" Cori snapped back into the moment.

"Is your kid missing?" Cori ignored her and pressed her head into the wall. "He'll tell me anyway."

"Why bother asking then?"

Gypsy shifted to the panel and pulled the stop button. Cori immediately tensed. Gypsy crossed her arms and leaned against the doors. "Something's wrong, and it isn't the usual prison-break stress."

"Do you really want to know?"

"I don't ask questions if I don't want the answers."

Cori stood up straight to face off with her. She holstered her gun and propped her hands on her hips. "Do you know—" Cori let out a mirthless chuckle. "Of course, you know. That's why you know as much as you do. Cleos. Geez, how stupid I've been." Cori rubbed her face.

"That wish reality where we met the first time," Cori continued. "When you went psycho and killed me." Gypsy nodded, being sure to maintain a passive expression so Cori didn't presume she felt anything resembling pride or amusement for the actions of her branched persona. "After you stabbed me—"

"She," Gypsy quickly corrected. "After *she* stabbed you..." Cori's brow dipped slightly, as if questioning why the distinction was necessary.

Cori clenched her teeth, apparently not ready to separate her memories from her reality. "I was choking on my own blood and I couldn't talk. I wasn't able to ask the genie for my penalties—not verbally, anyway. He had to bend the rules to help me. In recompense for the punishment he received for breaking those rules, he is calling in a debt. My son. He wants a life for a life."

Gypsy frowned. "The genie wants to kill your son?"

"No, he wants to become a human. He needs a body to do it, so he is going to use my son." A few tears trickled from Cori's eyes as she spoke. "He is fortunately giving me some time to acclimate to my circumstances."

Gypsy, despite many years in the supernatural world, knew very little about its details. Her priority, for personal and occupational reasons, had been to focus on werewolves. However, it didn't take a library of book knowledge for her to understand that fighting with the decree of a genie was futile.

"So, you can imagine how inopportune the timing of your arrival is," Cori said through barely contained rage.

"I'm sorry," Gypsy whispered.

Cori laughed and shook her head. "Are you? Are you capable of that?"

Gypsy resisted the urge to defend herself on that front. She was generally a heartless person, but she always drew the line at violence against children. It wasn't a mandate that anyone had given to her; it just wasn't fair. Children are weak—therefore they should be protected until such time when they can become a proper opponent. Plus, they were kind of cute.

"Maybe we arrived just in time. I'm sure Cleos will find something in the genie contracts that will prevent him from taking the child."

Cori laughed again. "We already have the solution, Gypsy."

"You do?"

"Yes. The child must be of warm flesh and no name to receive the energy of the universe." Cori air quoted.

"Then name him." Gypsy furrowed her brow, disappointed she had to point out such an obvious loophole.

"We can't. We've tried."

"That's ridiculous, just call him…" Gypsy trailed off as she tried to speak literally any name she could think of, but either because of some unseen edict or a lack of focus, she couldn't think of a single one. She couldn't even think of a random word to end her sentence with, so long as in her mind she considered it to be a name for the child. It reminded her of the way Cleos's mandates caused her anxiety and even discomfort when she tried to disobey them. Except this particular mental block didn't feel foreign to her. It felt as if it had existed in her mind since the day she was born. As odd as it was to be incapable of speaking a name, she also couldn't imagine any scenario in which Cori's child should have a name.

What would be the point?

"Don't bother," Cori said almost sympathetically as she watched Gypsy struggling to make her tongue push out a word. "The more you try, the more it slips away. It doesn't matter now, anyway. He's already been claimed. That's why we never named him. It didn't seem odd until now. It's like we were never meant to keep him," she said more to herself than Gypsy.

"If you can't name him, then what other…" Gypsy trailed off, as she remembered the first half of the statement. The child must be of warm flesh.

Gypsy felt her shoulders sink as if she had to bear the burden of this knowledge physically because she couldn't carry it emotionally.

"That's right," Cori said when it was clear Gypsy was on the same page. "I have until the end of twilight tonight to stop a demigod from possessing my son, or he will be executed. All because you're a fucking psychopath." Cori moved to the panel and pushed the stop button so the elevator could continue.

Gypsy slammed her hand against the wall behind Cori, effectively blocking her into the corner of the elevator. Cori pressed the muzzle of her pistol into her stomach, but Gypsy didn't draw back or pull her own weapon. This wasn't the time to get into this, but clearly, there would never be a better time. "All because *she* was a fucking psychopath," she corrected again.

Astonishment dragged Cori's mouth open. "Do you really think it makes a difference?"

"I am not the woman who did those things to you."

"You are one bad day away from being her, and I am the only one who can see it."

Gypsy shook her head slowly. "No, you aren't the only one who can see it." Her lips curled up into a sadistic smirk she knew would ignite Cori's fuse. Despite the gun being pressed into her stomach, the woman didn't pull the trigger. She did, however, headbutt her.

4

"WHO?" DANATO STARED BLANKLY across the elevator at Ethan. "Why would Renee saddle us with a former prisoner as a—never mind, I've answered my own question." He rubbed his temples, thinking about how much trouble Cleos was going to cause him. Forget that he could read the minds of 99.9% of the prison's occupants and staff. He was more concerned with the animosity that accompanied a man of his character. There was only so much unadulterated pomposity people could take. If Cleos was going to be freely roaming the prison, Danato was going to have to warn the staff about his personality.

"That's not all," Ethan continued. "He brought Gypsy and Leona with him."

Danato felt the blood drain from his face as he calculated how many hours it had been since the contentiously designated end of the full moon. "Cleos brought a fem-wolf to this facility less than 24 hours after her change?"

"She seems to be in pretty good condition." The elevator *ponked* as it arrived on the infirmary level and opened its doors. "Actually, she's in excellent condition," Ethan amended.

"The only good condition for a fem-wolf is pregnant," Danato muttered as he left the lift. As he turned to go to the infirmary entrance he nearly ran into the back of Leona. She turned slowly to face him and regarded him with wide eyes.

"Is that so?" she asked. Her lips pursed with disapproval.

"Leona." Danato swallowed hard. Though he towered over the woman, there was something about her—even beyond his knowledge of her strength—that made him uncomfortable. He imagined it was only his male ego—rejecting the idea that he was not the strongest person in the room. Though he made great efforts not to use his strength as a form of punishment, it was still nice to know he could at any time suppress the will of anyone around him. Anyone except a fem-wolf. "Ethan and I were just discussing our concerns for your health so soon after your change."

"My health? Or my mood?"

"I'm certain both are..." Danato trailed off as he began to notice the "excellent condition" Ethan had referred to. Never mind her beauty or the outrageous outfit, which advertised her assets like a hooker. The werewolf before him—just one day following a massive expansion in her muscular structure—was not retaining water as she should be. Her skin—which would have stretched to accommodate her inhuman body—wasn't pekid or shedding. If he hadn't known better, he would have assumed she hadn't even transformed. "How are you walking?" Danato backed away, examining her legs, which showed no sign of bowing. "And in heels no less? Your bones should be rubber," he said in disbelief. His eyes narrowed at her. "This is impossible."

Leona nodded. "Indeed, it is, but we can discuss the changes in my lunar cycle another time."

"Changes?" Danato felt himself tense, and he even took a step away from the fem-wolf.

Leona sighed and shook her head at Danato. "Relax, Danato, it's nothing that can endanger you. You might even be pleased with how progressive the Council of the Moon is being."

"I don't like anything progressive," Danato grumbled.

"Never mind then. That's not what I came here for. I came because we need to discuss an alliance."

"An alliance?" Danato perked his brow. "What do you need now?"

"Actually, it is more about what I can do for you. We have mutual interests to explore."

"And somehow this involves my former prisoner?"

"Oh yes, Cleos is the one who enlightened me on the potential for our collaboration. He is predicting major changes in the prison hierarchy." Danato glanced at Ethan. He didn't consider Cleos a reliable source for fortune-telling since most of his predictions were based on his knowledge of personalities rather than any actual prophetic ability. However, his business acumen had its own level of foresight, which he couldn't ignore. Knowing one's opponents was the key to predicting their future behavior.

And even if Danato wanted to deny the suggestion of corruption among his superiors, he couldn't. This wasn't the first time he had heard rumors of an upset in the ranks. Maddox had already warned him that the young members of the board didn't understand the need for the unprofitable institution.

"Our reciprocal cooperation may be the key to keeping this prison in its rightful hands," Leona said.

"And whose hands would you be referring to?"

Leona gave him an honest smile. "Yours, of course." She bowed her head slightly as if deferring some great power to him.

For a moment, he considered this scenario. He would be in charge of the prison—without anyone to report to. No paperwork. No rules. No structure. It would be a complete disaster. "What exactly does Cleos have in mind?"

"Change," Cleos said as he stepped out of the stairwell, followed shortly after by Efrat. Danato was surprised he had trudged down so many floors instead of using the elevator, but as he watched Cleos shield his face from the light, he wondered if the bright bulbs in the elevator were more of a deterrent than the physical strain on his knees.

"This place is in desperate need of new blood, new money, and a new purpose."

"You mean a purpose beyond locking away dangerous entities."

Cleos sighed and gave a sorrowful, almost pouty look to Leona. "Darling, would you mind fetching your parasol?" He turned his blinking and watering eyes toward the ceiling where the rays of harsh fluorescent lights were beating down on him. Even the short exposure was making his skin look pink—as if he were getting a sunburn. Had the prison been equipped with incandescent bulbs, Cleos would have already been getting welts. As it was, if he didn't get some kind of protection soon—his skin would develop blisters.

Leona leaned down and dug out a compact umbrella from her rolling suitcase. Cleos popped it open and shielded his face from the interior lights. "There, that's better. Now I can conduct our business comfortably."

"I'm still not convinced we have any business to conduct."

"Now, now, Danato. We mustn't let our past predict our future. Let bygones be bygones so we can all behave professionally."

The elevator *ponked* beside them and the doors opened. Gypsy launched backward from the lift with Cori facilitating her reverse. Both women were screeching and grunting as they landed on the floor, continuing their wrestling match outside of the confines of the carriage's contained space.

"Well, at least some of us can." Cleos pinched his face in disgust at the display.

"Both of you stop this!" Danato yelled.

With no regard for his order, Cori threw her fist into Gypsy's face. The resounding smack guaranteed the woman a bruised face. Gypsy flipped her off and pulled a small knife from her back pocket. Danato opened his mouth to warn Cori, but Cleos spoke before he could.

"Aah-aah-aah," Cleos sang, raising a chiding finger at his underling. Gypsy glared at him but dropped the knife before attacking Cori. She shoved her back, forcing her to stumble and land on her ass. It was hardly an equal response to the black eye Cori had given her, but Danato assumed Gypsy was more interested in playing with her like a cat than going in for the kill right away.

Ethan approached Cori, ready to intervene on her behalf. "Don't, Ethan!" Cori demanded. "Stay out of this!" Cori turned her attention to Danato, who was also creeping up on Gypsy, ready to put an end to the outburst. He recognized the frothing vengeance in her eyes, and he considered whether he would intervene in this fight if it were Ethan's vendetta. He decided to give Cori some leniency to exhaust her anger—at least until Gypsy got out of hand.

Cori stood, and the women danced a moment before beginning their punching match. Cori dodged a slow jab, while Gypsy deflected two more from Cori. She took one to the stomach and narrowly avoided a second black eye.

Gypsy spun around Cori and gave her a quick hit to her lower back. Cori barely winced at the contact, which could and should have brought her to her knees. Gypsy was no doubt considerably stronger than Cori and should have been capable of putting her down with a few well-placed punches. And yet she was the one with a bleeding nose and a blooming black eye. She was holding back. But why? Was she really capable of mercy? Or was she under orders not to hurt Cori?

Danato turned his attention to Cleos, who was watching the brawl with interest. When he noticed Danato's attention, he smiled mischievously at him. "Aren't you glad I'm one of the good guys?"

Danato frowned at that statement. He was glad to know Cleos had put some restrictions on Gypsy, but it was done with the type of authority that made Danato wonder if releasing Cleos was the right choice.

"I feel your judgment down to my toes, Danato," Cleos said.

"Perhaps you should call her off, so we can get on with this," Danato suggested.

"Certainly," Cleos said with a glimmer of delight in his eyes. "Corinthia, stop!"

The moment the words were out, Cori stopped her attack on Gypsy. Danato stared at the spectacle of his normally contentious subordinate being abruptly obedient. However, the mixture of shock and fear in her eyes sent a shiver down Danato's spine. Cori hadn't acted by choice. Cleos had commanded her, and without question, she had obeyed.

"What the hell did you just do?" Danato could hear a tremor in his voice, but he had to know the truth.

"Oh, I'm sorry, did you mean the other one?"

Danato grabbed onto Cleos's suit jacket and yanked him onto his tippy toes. "You knew damn well what I meant. Since when have you been able to control her like that?"

Cleos looked at him with mocking disbelief. "What on earth do you mean? I'm quite certain Cori has complete control of her faculties. Just like you do. Now let me go."

Danato released Cleos, letting him drop to the floor. Even after he did it, he couldn't tell if he had done it voluntarily or if Cleos had ordered him to do it. Another shiver ran along his spine, but this time it was out of anger instead of fear. He narrowed his gaze on Cleos.

The photophobe straightened his suit jacket and stepped in close to Danato, holding the umbrella over both their heads as he spoke. "You've always underestimated me, Danato. But perhaps now is the time for you to consider how much of an asset I could be working beside you instead of against you." He shifted back and waved at Leona. "Come along, dear. Let's get this meeting underway before we are all reduced to savages." He gave

Gypsy a look of disdain that she rolled her eyes at. She wiped the blood from her nose and followed them.

Danato looked back at Ethan and Cori, who looked just as worried by this development as he was. However, since Cleos hadn't used this power until now, he assumed it was for one of two reasons. Either it was a very difficult task to accomplish or he really wasn't interested in controlling the actions of every person he met.

Just some of them.

5

D ANATO TOOK THE HEAD seat at the table in the meeting room just off the nurses' hub in the infirmary. Cleos and Leona sat on his left and right. Belus arrived late and took a seat beside Cleos. He instructed Efrat to sit next to Leona, a power play that was not entirely lost on the fem-wolf.

It displeased Danato to see that Gypsy was perfectly comfortable sitting at the head of the table opposite him with Cori and Ethan flanking her. Her casual manner of lounging reminded him of Daniel. The momentary association made his heart ache. His death was still fresh in their thoughts, but with so many other matters pressing them onward, no one had a chance to mourn him properly. Least of all Ethan, who was persevering dutifully—albeit numbly. It wasn't a change Danato could be happy about. Quiet pain was a sorrow demon's favorite food.

As everyone settled into their chairs, Danato noticed Cori had pulled her chair a significant distance from Efrat. He had forgotten about him in relation to her rings. He could no longer touch her without hurting her. A caveat that was probably for the best given their quarrelsome relationship. However, Danato was certain this would be yet another challenge to the elemental's efforts to have a semi-normal life. It was bad enough he was now without Duke—the man with whom he had found some common ground.

Danato could never have predicted Duke would eventually try to release Riley, thereby encasing himself in stone. But he should have known that bringing the Medusa statue out into the light would dredge up old memories. Regardless of Duke's understanding of the statue's lure—it ultimately would have been his needling guilt that caused him to succumb to the quiet siren's call.

If no one had witnessed the exchange, Danato would have been tempted to put Riley right back in it. He could have lied to Duke and told him the statue rejected him for some unknown reason. That was what he still wanted to do, but he couldn't risk the potential fallout from such an antagonistic act. As it was, there was another problem threatening to pull his humanity right out from beneath him. But he couldn't think about that. Not yet.

"Can we dim the lights so I don't have to hold this umbrella the whole time?" Cleos asked. Ethan went back to the switch and dimmed the lights to a mood-lighting level. "Thank you." Cleos lowered his umbrella to the floor.

"Let's get on with this," Danato prompted as soon as Ethan sat down. "Why the hell are you back in my prison with a werewolf and a…" Danato held back his accusation of sociopath, but judging by the smile and wink he got from Gypsy, she already knew what he intended to say.

"Maybe I should let Leona start." Cleos waved to his accomplice.

Leona bobbed her head respectfully at him. "As you know, I am the leader of the Council of the Moon now. Unlike my predecessor, I am exploring a more expansive definition of werewolf. By including half and quarter breeds into our community, I feel it will strengthen our connection to our heritage rather than disseminate it. I'm interested in being more than just a pack of wild dogs. You asked me earlier, Danato, how I could be here less than 24 hours after my change and still be functional—and beautiful." Leona added, drawing a little chuckle from Cleos. "The answer is that I did not change."

"What do you mean?" Danato stared at her awestruck. Not changing was impossible for a werewolf. Although the lunar cycle coincided with the metamorphosis, it was still an internal mechanism that instigated the change. Regardless of where they lived, werewolves all around the world began their change at the same time—or within minutes of each other. There were, of course, variations in the duration of the change and the speed of their diminishing mental faculties, but that had more to do with age. Ultimately, the one thing that unified all werewolves, male and female, was the change. That was why so many werewolves did not consider half-breeds to be true werewolves. Without that burden of pain—they were just moody humans.

"I mean just what I said," Leona continued. "I endured a partial transformation that was substantially less trying on my muscles and caused little to no skin resurfacing. But I did not reach a full transition."

"And just how exactly did you accomplish that?" asked Belus.

Leona turned her attention to his second. "My people and I have been experimenting with stunting our hormones. The results have been extremely favorable. I believe within a matter of months or at least years we may be able to identify and counter all the hormones that lead to our excessive anatomical expansion."

"You want to bypass the change altogether." Danato verified. "Doesn't that go against your heritage?"

Leona shrugged. "There will be opposition to our endeavor. People who believe that the change is essential to being a separate species. However, the truth is, that we will always be werewolves. We will have superior strength and speed. Better hearing and olfactory senses than humans. The change isn't necessary. The change is not who we are. It's just a burden we must bear. I feel, as many of my followers do, that our community would be best supported by increasing the longevity of our lives and reducing the guilt and humiliation that such a violent and bloodthirsty alter ego affords us."

Danato sat back in his chair and looked Leona over. This was not what he had expected. An ardent, heartfelt argument for genuine change. Empathy for both full and part werewolves. Either Leona had changed, or she was putting on a magnificent show of diplomacy. "I think that sounds like a very agreeable change. I don't envy the long journey you have ahead of you, but it sounds promising."

"Thank you," Leona smiled warmly.

"If you don't mind my asking, what does that have to do with my prison—other than fewer dollars going into my pocket for housing?"

"One frustration that comes with being a werewolf living inside of the real world is that we can't be open about who we are. We have to hide our strength and speed, especially the females." Leona rolled her eyes, drawing a smirk from Danato. As someone who regularly downplayed his strength, he understood what she meant. "We have few opportunities to openly exert our full potential without drawing attention to ourselves. It's because of this that I believe my sister wanted to venerate our change and minimize acceptance to only those who have to endure it. If I want my people to accept a life that my sister would've considered demeaning, I have to give them something in return."

"And what exactly is that?" Danato asked.

"I want to reestablish the connection between the werewolf population and this facility, as well as its subsidiary factions."

Danato's brow creased with confusion. "You want to work for me?"

Leona waggled her head. "I would qualify it more as... freelance work, but yes. I want my people to be your hunters."

Danato shifted back in his chair, considering this idea for a moment. This was not a new idea, but rather an old idea rehashed. The only reason werewolves stopped being hunters in the first place was because they kept killing the criminals that they were supposed to be delivering for incarceration. "If this hormone replacement works, do you anticipate your brethren to be less volatile?"

"Since the therapy disrupts the cycle, the remaining days have significantly fewer peaks. Our young werewolves will have the temperament of an older wolf, and our older wolves may have as much control as a human. So, there will no longer be an issue with safe delivery. And since werewolves are better equipped for the work—you reduce your loss of life."

"That all sounds good, but I don't hire the hunters myself. Why didn't you take this to one of our recruiters?"

"Because not only are your recruiters no longer recruiting," Cleos interjected. "They will soon be without jobs themselves."

"What do you mean?" Danato asked.

Cleos tipped his head to one side, examining Danato. "I think you know exactly what I am talking about. You and I both have had our suspicions for a while. The only difference is I have a clear view of the thought processes behind the scenes. This place is teetering on the edge. No one wants to put the money in anymore, and unless I can find a way for you to start producing money, you'll all be broke by the end of the year. And we all know what happens when the money runs out."

"Are you suggesting that you will help finance the prison?" Belus asked.

"It's not that simple. Even I don't have an endless supply of money. Though it wouldn't be difficult to achieve, I am *trying to* stay out of a prison cell."

"That's a first," Cori muttered.

Cleos shifted to look down at Cori. "I was never interested in staying in my cell, I just wasn't happy about the method it took to get me out."

"Once again, I can't be held responsible for what the rings did."

"The rings gave you the ability, but it was your nosy curiosity that put you in my mind."

"My nosy curiosity is the only reason you're sitting at this table as an equal instead of downstairs in a cell."

"I didn't leave because my prison sentence was over. I left because I thought it was the only way to save you from yourself."

"What is that supposed to mean?" Cori dipped her brow.

"It means that I had never intended to be sitting at this table. It would've been for the best if we had never seen each other again. But something changed. Something that I couldn't ignore, so, *once again*, I am back in your life to save your ass."

"Out of the goodness of your heart or your pocketbook?"

"If you had any idea how much you need me, you ungrateful little brat!" Cleo rose from his chair. "You wouldn't dare speak to me like this!"

"You're so lucky my rings aren't working!"

"Oh, I am keenly aware of your impudent rings. I couldn't be happier to have you out of my mind and back to your powerless old self again. I rejoice in your impuissance."

Efrat reached out his hand, throwing a trickle of electricity into the light above Cleos. The room immediately brightened, and the amplified light sent Cleos ducking for safety beneath his arms.

A deafening shot rang out in the room. The light above shattered, raining shrapnel down on Cleos and everyone around him.

Ethan jumped from his seat and whipped out his weapon. He held the gun on Gypsy, who was already blowing the smoke off her muzzle. She didn't seem the least bit ruffled by having Ethan's gun pointed at her temple. Nor was she riled by the need to use her gun, to begin with.

"Enough!" Danato slammed his fists down on the meeting table, shattering its plastic veneer. He was happy to at least make a few people jump, though not the ones he would've preferred. "This childish bickering has gone on long enough. Cleos, whatever your issues are with Cori, you need to get them figured out because there will be no place for you here if you don't. Regardless of what offers you have to bring to the table. I'm ashamed to say that the only one in this room who seems to be behaving themselves is the goddamn werewolf."

Leona let out a quiet scoff and shifted uncomfortably. She obviously didn't like being pointed out as *the good one*.

"I can hardly conduct any business with everyone reacting to every little argument that they have with violence. That goes double for you, Efrat, and triple for you, Gypsy. Now all of you get out!"

Danato watched as Cori left the table sullen, with Efrat right behind her. Gypsy didn't move until she had gotten the okay from Cleos, who gave her a curt nod as permission. Ethan graciously escorted her to the door with his hand on his recently holstered gun.

"Now," Danato said, regaining the civility in his voice. "Where were we?" He sat back down, noting the smirk on Leona's face. She reached forward, touching the crack in the table that he had created.

"We were just explaining to you how much we need each other right now."

6

"Way to go, Bolt." Gypsy patted Efrat on the back. "You got us all kicked out."

"Me? You're the one acting like Charles Bronson in there."

"Speaking of." Ethan reached around Gypsy and ripped her gun from her holster. She tried to grab it back, but he grabbed her reaching hand and pushed his thumb into the bone until it felt like it was going to break. She ripped her hand back and rubbed the affected area.

"I'll be getting that back soon enough," she said.

"You'll get it back when I say you get it back. The last time you were here, you proved your hero status. Now it's time to prove you can be a team player. That is assuming your employment with Cleos will be long-standing and that we will be seeing more of you."

"You should know that I've never played well with others."

"Then I'm sure you can find your way to the door."

"I'm sure I could, but unfortunately I'm tethered to the princess in there."

"Leona?"

"Her too."

"I'll be in the office if anyone needs me," Cori murmured and left the infirmary.

Gypsy watched her go. She had hoped to continue their brawl away from the prying eyes of the grownups. However, since she couldn't force her fists past the confines of her programmed edicts, it was probably best that Cori saved her the humiliation of a second black eye. Still, she had rather enjoyed stretching her legs with the woman. Perhaps when the world wasn't collapsing around her, Cori would be up for a rematch.

"Cori told me about the baby situation." Gypsy looked back at Ethan. His face hardened, as if he expected a punch. She was certain he would have preferred it. "What can I do?" she asked.

"Pardon?"

Gypsy shrugged. "We'll be here through tomorrow. I might as well do something useful while I'm here. Downtime isn't wise for a person with my proclivities. Without an agenda, I'm liable to shoot or fuck someone I'm not supposed to." Gypsy took the opportunity to admire his physique. She knew Ethan was off limits, but much as anything in life—she didn't readily take no for an answer. "And you just took my gun away."

Ethan didn't seem flustered by her attention. He was probably used to being ogled by the staff. "You want to be useful? Stay away from Cori. And don't piss off Danato." Ethan headed to the door.

"That's not productive," Gypsy called after him.

"Efrat, you mind watching our guest for a while?"

Efrat furrowed his brow and huffed out his breath. "Yes, sir."

Gypsy smirked at Efrat once Ethan was gone. "Well, well, well, back to you and me again." Gypsy sauntered closer to him and dragged her finger down his chest. "And not an ex-boyfriend in sight to interrupt."

Efrat batted her hand away before it could make it past his waistline. "You do realize the more excited I get, the more electric I get. It makes intimacy rather difficult."

Gypsy looked over his hands and nodded. This was one case in point where she needed to take no for an answer. It was a damn shame, but probably for the best. "That's alright. I don't think you and I are meant to be friends with benefits, anyway."

"Is that so?"

Gypsy nodded. "Not so long as you find me so wholly unattractive."

Efrat's face muddled as he gave her a quick once-over. "Well, I'm sure there's an attractive lesbian in there somewhere."

Gypsy chuckled. "Oh, there it is. The blatant prejudice that demands you find authoritative women masculine is hindering your sex life, you know? You can't tell me you wouldn't enjoy being dominated by a strong woman. Maybe not me..." Gypsy glanced toward the door. "...but someone."

"If a werewolf can't dominate me, what makes you think... someone else could?"

"Oh please, Efrat. You're already in chains. I saw how you came to her rescue when Cleos insulted her. That's more than her husband did."

"Ethan has expectations of behavior."

"And you don't."

"Not that anyone expects me to live up to."

Gypsy stepped closer to him. He stiffened and stretched his hands out to keep from shocking her. "It seems to me that with Duke gone, you might have a lot more expectations put on you. Are you ready for that, Efrat? Are you ready to be the hero instead of the villain?"

Efrat's eyes fluttered over her face. "I was never the villain."

Gypsy smiled. "People like us—the ones who don't live up to those expectations of behavior—are always the villains in their eyes." Gypsy leaned in closer despite it being a terrible idea. "Rebels. Instigators. Trouble-makers." She tipped her head up to meet his lips.

"Please don't," he whispered.

Gypsy was close enough to feel his heat and the increasing surge from his hands. She noted the throbbing vessel in his neck and the bob of his Adam's apple as he swallowed. Up close, he smelled remarkably like ozone. She wanted more than anything to take a bite out of him in more ways than one, but she knew he wasn't pleading for her to stop because he didn't want her. He was pleading because every step he took toward pleasure—ultimately meant more pain for him and her.

Gypsy abruptly drew back and gave him a hard cuff on the shoulder that made him wobble. "You're right. Sex isn't the right move for either of us right now. I think you and I are meant to be buddies."

Efrat scoffed. "Really? You and me?"

"Yup, I'm just the right kind of crazy to keep your cynical side from tipping into asshole territory."

"I think you're about seven years too late for that."

Gypsy shrugged. "Sorry, I got here as fast as I could."

"And what do I get out of this little friendship?"

Gypsy considered that a moment. Without providing sex or protection, she honestly wasn't sure that she had anything to contribute to an alliance with Efrat.

Gypsy snapped her fingers. "I know where the best liquor is."

7

"LET'S CUT THE BULLSHIT, Cleos." Danato leaned back in his chair until the weak plastic complained at the pressure. "What do you want?"

"I've told you what I want."

"To study hundred-year-old mirrors and dolls? Possibly. I can see some potential for profit in anti-aging and fertility, but there are easier ways to break into the pharmaceutical racket. You've obviously gone to great lengths to get Leona in command of the werewolves." Danato nodded toward Leona. The fem-wolf flashed a contented smile at Cleos. "How expensive are coups these days?"

Cleos gave Danato a sour look. "You don't want to know."

"No, I probably don't, but what I do need to know is what this is going to cost me. What are you going to get from this alliance?"

"It's not numbers I'm after, Danato. It's power."

Danato clenched his jaw. "What kind of power?"

Cleos blanched and shook his head vigorously. "No, no, no. Not that kind of power." Cleos folded his hands in his lap. "As you said, let's cut the bullshit? You and I both know that a takeover is imminent. The fuckwit grandchildren who are now coming onto the board are shutting things down from the outside in. I don't have an exact date, but I know when they do come in, it will be fast and bloody. There won't be time to defend your heritage like there was with the Russians."

"And why should we believe you?" Belus asked.

Cleos slowly turned his head to glare at the small man next to him. He turned back to Danato and extended an open hand to him. "I'm an open book. If you care to read me."

Danato was familiar with Cleos's form of memory transference. He wasn't particularly interested in seeing through the psychic's eyes. Besides that, he didn't need proof that Cleos was speaking the truth. He knew this day would eventually come. The day when someone else tried to take the prison from him. He shouldn't have cared. He should have just walked away now and gone into hiding. He would live longer if he did.

But he had obligations.

"You still haven't told me what you want."

"I want the board dissolved. I want the threat eliminated, and I want Danato Calibria on his throne where he belongs."

"You want me to continue to run a prison with no funding and no one to cover it up."

"Please." Cleos scoffed. "I can make this prison disappear overnight. Replacing the board will be as easy as a handshake and long overdue. Unfortunately, I can't be responsible for perpetually funding this place, so we need to find something more useful to produce than empty boxes. And of course, I have no intention of babysitting this operation. Aside from the dreadful climate and lacking amenities, I don't particularly like any of you. So, while I am gone, I will need an experienced and dedicated overseer. Who better to monitor things back here than the man already prepared to serve a life sentence?"

"You want me to work for you."

"I agree that it's a sideways move for you—from one unnamed authority to another. However, I am entirely certain that you are the only man capable of keeping this place from going up in flames." The small smile on his face turned to a sneer, and he opened his mouth almost reluctantly—as if he loathed to speak his next words. "There is one aspect of this arrangement that you may not like, but I feel it's necessary, in the interest of partnership, to give you prior warning about the change."

"And what change is that?" Danato asked, his voice already reaching a level of threat.

Cleos hesitated, his hands clenched anxiously. Danato had not expected such a display from the egotistical man. He either didn't like the change that he had to make or he already knew what Danato's reaction to it would be.

Cleos took a breath and hardened his expression into something resembling his normal pompous self. "I will be relocating Cori to a branch facility in America."

Danato's gaze shifted into a blurred trance that he was certain was the onset of a blackout rage. The words being spoken had no meaning to Danato. It all just translated to a single emotion. A level of grief that was comparable to the day he lost his wife. A feeling that was no doubt compounded by the threat looming just beyond the twilight and his responsibility to stop it.

Danato lunged at the waxy white face before him—prepared to shove him to the floor. There would be no danger of him retaliating with his mind because Cleos's head would be shrapnel before he could touch him or speak to him. A man's blood would spray the walls of this prison for the second time in such a short span.

Danato's leap went irreversibly sideways. The burning pain in his shoulder barely registered before his hip hit the ground. Leona's weight pressed down on him, pushing his shoulders back flat against the white-tiled floor. Her skinny legs clamped onto his torso, squeezing his belly and forcing air from his lungs. It was still jarring to him to feel the strength of a Mack truck coming from such a small frame. She had no doubt smelled his attack and tackled him to prevent him from killing Cleos.

Danato grabbed her by the waist and lifted her. Despite her clamped knees and her abnormally heavy body, he threw her off him. She hit the wall of the meeting room and rebounded before he could get off the floor.

She jumped back on him, and her pelvis punched him in the stomach. He groaned and grappled with her hands as she, in turn, tried to pin him down. When she finally got a grip, she pressed down on him, trapping his wrists next to his head. Beyond the emasculation of it all, Danato found it even more grating that she was doing it to defend Cleos. Didn't Leona know she was just a puppet to him?

They were all puppets to him.

"Get off him, Leona," Belus said, still sounding calm while his boss brawled on the floor like the erratic subordinates he had just kicked out of the office.

"Do as he says, Leona," Cleos rasped urgently.

Leona looked up at him, and her eyes widened. Her face contorted with disbelief. Reluctantly, she dismounted her prey and stood.

Once Danato was upright, he observed the tiny dagger pressed into Cleos's neck. It was not technically a threat, since the blade had already punctured his carotid artery. Danato could see a rivulet of blood coming out of the wound like a tiny, pulsing waterfall. All Belus had to do was twist, and the man would be in danger of exsanguination. Because Belus was one of the very few humans immune to his mental sovereignty, he was a legitimate threat to the man.

It was the equivalent of the great and powerful Oz being brought down by a munchkin, and no one was more aware of that than Cleos himself. It would be yet another reason for him to despise Belus.

Danato leaned into Cleos, getting a close-up view of his flaring nostrils before he spoke. "If we both come out alive on the other side of this siege, we can discuss sharing the responsibility of this prison. Beyond that... I have nothing else to offer you."

Cleos hissed as Belus removed the blade. He immediately pressed his hands to his neck, staunching the blood flow.

"See the doctor." Danato turned to leave and found himself chest to breast with Leona. She looked more than a little put out by this turn of the tables. After a momentary standoff, she eased away from him and leaned against the meeting table. He heard the veneer crack further as her hands squeezed the lip of the table. He moved past her, meeting Belus at the door.

"I meant what I said to her earlier," Cleos called after him.

Danato paused at the door and exchanged a glance with Belus. Neither of them remembered what he had said earlier.

"I'm here to help," he clarified.

Danato wasn't sure that Cleos was speaking in earnest. For all his power to see into the minds of others, Cleos was still a selfish creature. His compassion for Cori was most likely limited to his affinity for the flavor of her mind and what it would take to possess it.

And even now—facing the dire situation that he had stumbled upon—Danato was certain Cleos was trying to protect his investment more than her. The prison had been on the precipice of falling apart even before the board ripped it apart. If he didn't do something to repair the damage, then there would be no one left to run his money-making machine.

However, Danato didn't have the luxury of pride in this situation. If there was the slightest chance that Cleos could be useful to them, he had to accept that offer. They all wanted to protect Cori's son. To save him—from the gods... and the monsters.

8

EFRAT STOOD IN THE doorway of the house, reluctant to enter. Gypsy, on the other hand, marched in without concern for the house's wrath. She looked back at Efrat and smirked at him. "What do you think she's gonna do—swallow you up and spit you out?"

"I've heard rumors."

"Mmm." Gypsy ignored his concerns and moved to the hidden panel beside the fireplace. She chuckled as she looked over the fine collection of liquor. She wasn't a connoisseur of alcohol. To her, beer was beer, whiskey was whiskey, and tequila was trouble. She pulled out a full bottle of vodka and decided it was likely the least expensive alcohol to snatch. She felt static sparks hitting her back and turned partway to find Efrat standing right behind her.

"I'm pretty sure this is the type of thing I'm supposed to prevent."

"Yup, but I don't think you're going to."

"And why is that?"

"Because you like me."

Efrat nearly choked with laughter. "I actually *don't* like you."

"That is exactly why you like me."

"What?" Efrat furrowed his brow.

"Listen." Gypsy turned the rest of the way to face him. "There are two types of men in my life. Ones I fuck and ones I don't. You, my friend, are the type that I don't."

Efrat's jaw rolled. She recognized the debate on his face. Was her evaluation of their lack of chemistry an insult or a relief? Gypsy knew that her features and physique combined with her brazen personality put many men on the fence. Efrat just needed to commit to one side or the other so they could move on.

"So, that automatically makes us best friends?" he asked, disinterest returning to his face.

"No, but neither does fucking. You and I are going to be friends because I don't give a shit about your problems. I'm not going to sit here and listen to you whinge about your pathetic life and how you're never going to be normal, never going to get the girl, and never going to leave this prison ever again. The truth is, if I could trade places with you, I'd be happy to have the power of a thunderstorm at my fingertips. There's a lot I could do with that much power."

"Power isn't everything," he said acridly.

"It's worth a lot to me."

"More than human contact?" he asked.

Gypsy swirled her finger over her face, exhibiting the flat expression it held. "Do you see this? This is me not giving a fuck about your shit. I stand by what I said. It's just fortunate for both of us that no one is stupid enough to give me that much power."

"And what would you do with it if someone were stupid enough?"

Gypsy smirked mischievously. "I have lists."

"Oh, sure, revenge, but then what?"

"I have long lists." Gypsy lost her smile, and Efrat paused on her features, recognizing that little part of her that made Callin finally shrink away from her. The part that put Cori on edge. The part that didn't quite fit in with the rest of the human race.

Efrat took the bottle from her and moved to the couch. "So why did you bring me here if not for sex or to listen to my woes?"

"To drink."

Efrat set the bottle on the coffee table and carefully rested his elbows on his knees, keeping his hands away from the fabric of the couch. "Something tells me that you would have had no qualms about helping yourself to Danato's stash, with or without company. Why don't we just skip the bullshit and go straight to the horns?"

Gypsy frowned. "Nobody ever lets me do things my way around here." She took the bottle back off the coffee table and twisted the top off. She took a heavy swig before settling into the big chair behind her. She felt a sharp spring poking her ass, but she ignored it.

She looked over Efrat before speaking as frankly as she could without divulging her employer's secrets. Not that she knew many of them. He did so like his drama, and part of that drama was the surprises. She hated the unknown. It was a damn sloppy way to work.

"Do you know anything about Cleos?"

Efrat's eyes skirted the floor as if recollecting conversations he had had about him. To her knowledge, Cleos and Efrat hadn't interacted much or at all during his stint in the prison. "I know he's a mind reader."

"That's an understatement," Gypsy mumbled. "I'll sum up the resume for you. Cleos comes from a very distinguished breed of psychics. Very distinguished," Gypsy mocked Cleos' condescending tone. "He is one of very few readers who can imbibe and reconstitute memories. However, his skills don't just stop at memory lane. He has an innate understanding of how these memories have shaped a person's character. As a result, he can reshape personalities, and nullify specific character traits. He can rewire the brain to think and therefore react differently. He can essentially reprogram the human mind. Or in worst-case scenarios, he can just outright lobotomize them."

"And he can do that just by touching someone."

"He can get a pretty decent read on a stranger just from a single touch. From someone he knows already, he can change their world with the briefest touch." Efrat frowned. "Rest assured, the lobotomy takes a little longer." Gypsy winked at him.

Efrat allowed a shimmer of a smirk to pass over his lips. "When he touched me earlier, on the roof... What was that about?"

Gypsy shrugged. "Probably just getting a general read on you."

"He said I could thank him later."

Gypsy nodded. "Cleos has a proposition for you."

"What kind of proposition?"

"A business proposition."

"What does he want?"

"Loyalty for one, but that's never optional under his employ. A lot of changes will be taking place in the prison in the coming months."

"So I've heard. What does that have to do with me?"

Gypsy chuckled. "Oh, that's cute you're modest."

"Excuse me."

"Efrat, if you weren't so blinded by your own shit, you would realize you're quite possibly the strongest elemental ever to exist. Your creation, albeit an aberration of science and magic, has serendipitously made you into a walking, talking bolt of lightning."

Efrat stared blankly at her—disinterested in her evaluation, regardless of how complimentary it was. "And your boss wants to use me for what?"

Gypsy considered her answer for a moment. She was getting better at obfuscation to trick her mental blocks, but Cleos hadn't closed as many doors on her this time. He must have known that Efrat would require some explanation for his sudden interest in the elemental. She took another swig of the vodka in her hand and looked into the fire. "There's a war coming."

Efrat didn't speak for a long moment. He sighed and cleared his throat. "What kind of war?" He sounded perturbed, as if she were offering a sales pitch instead of a warning.

Gypsy looked back at him. "The kind of war that you were designed to fight."

Efrat's eyes widened slightly. She had his attention now, but the narrowed eyes of a perpetually distrustful man followed the fleeting moment of realization on his face. "I didn't free myself from Clark just to be put under another man's thumb. It's bad enough that Danato has such a firm grip on my balls right now."

"No thumbs. No grips. We aren't asking you to be a weapon, Efrat. Just a soldier. We want you to be what you were intended to be."

"I was intended to be a man fighting on behalf of the United States of America."

Gypsy shook her head. "Country lines will mean nothing in this war."

"Who exactly will be starting this war?"

"Most likely the Russians, but he also suspects there may be a branch of the board going rogue. Members who still believe in the value of the prison, but only for themselves. He's aware of several factions around the world that would be happy to control the prison."

"Control the prison, or control the bubble?"

Gypsy's only answer was to smile. "It's vital that we get your fidelity before there are any altercations."

"You want to know if I'm loyal to the prison?"

"I know you're not loyal to the prison, but you are loyal to Cori. So, the question is, can you be loyal even if Cori is not on your side?"

"What is that supposed to mean?" Efrat's gaze narrowed on her, but her restrictions kept her from saying anything more.

"There are still a lot of things Cleos doesn't know. The least of which is when this is all going to go down, but that's why we're here. He needs to get a grip on this prison before someone else does."

"I'm not sure if I'm reading you right. Are you saying that my loyalties should lie with Cleos instead of Danato?"

Gypsy stared at Efrat unblinking. She offered him nothing. She couldn't. Not yet. Not until Cleos was convinced of his allegiance.

"What makes you think that I would consider this? From everything you just told me, Cleos could be detrimental to my mental health."

Gypsy nodded and took another swig of the vodka. She was just feeling good. That perfect tipsy place where she was relaxed but still capable of pulling a knife if need be. "He will pay handsomely for your faithfulness."

Efrat snorted. "The richest man at Shawshank. Thanks, but I think I'll stay on Danato's good side and keep my head on my shoulders." Efrat stood and rounded the couch to the front door.

"Not money, Efrat. He can fix you," Gypsy added. Her words slurred a little, but it didn't matter. He understood her just fine.

Efrat stopped in his tracks. Blue rivulets coursed up his arms, blackening his shirt sleeves. He turned his head only to look at her. "What did you say?" She could see he wasn't the type of man to dangle carrots in front of. Not without getting her fingers bitten off.

"You weren't listening earlier, were you? Cleos can reprogram the human brain. He can rewire you, Efrat. He can give those hands an off switch."

The anger melted from Efrat's eyes, replaced by something only seen in small children on Christmas morning. Though he would certainly debate the morality of deposing the warden a good deal longer, she was certain he had already decided. And that was the only answer that mattered to Cleos.

9

D ANATO SAT IN HIS office and rubbed his face. He was still taking in the revelations of the earlier meeting. Never in a million years would he have considered teaming up with a fem-wolf to bring back the old days of hunter recruitment. Nor could he imagine Cleos as his superior.

He had been so angry about Cleos presuming he could transfer Cori that he hadn't asked any questions. Namely—why he wanted to relocate her? Why would he take her from her home and her family? Would Ethan and...

Danato's thoughts stalled as he realized that soon there would be no more *and*. Life as he knew it was about to change. Perhaps that was why Cleos planned to move her away. She would no longer want to stay at the prison. Not after...

A small tap on the door disrupted his thoughts further. He looked up and saw Leona in the frame. The small smile on her face seemed innocent enough, but he still tensed. He couldn't tell if she was planning to continue their spat. After all, she hadn't officially won yet. He was still conscious. "What is it?" he asked dismissively.

"Am I disturbing you?"

Danato looked down at his desk, wondering what he had originally intended to do. He saw the genie contract and cringed. He needed to read it again, but he had already read it a hundred times. He knew what the answer was. They all knew what the answer was.

Still...

He would read it again. He would stare at the words on the page intensely, hoping to find new meaning in the only elaboration they could find on the genie's actions. All the while, a mixture of images would swirl around in his head, fighting to block out a frighteningly close future. A future that left him with no grandson—and possibly no relationship with his successors.

History was repeating itself in the worst way possible.

"No," he said, shoving the paper out of sight.

"I wanted to check on you." Leona came inside and stood at the edge of his desk.

"Check on me?" he asked.

"Your wrists." She raised her own hands, showing him her own delicate wrists. "I don't always know my own strength."

"Oh." He rubbed the bluish skin on one of his wrists. The outline of Leona's grip made it look like he had been in shackles for weeks. "It's nothing. Superficial. It won't last long."

"Side effect of the dragon serum?" she asked.

"Yes," he admitted.

"Handy stuff." He grunted in agreement. "Werewolves can't digest it, you know?"

Danato furrowed his brow and shook his head. "No, I didn't know that. I suppose that's for the best. It's not like we need werewolves any stronger."

Leona laughed—or rather, she giggled. The mirthful sound amazed Danato. He wasn't aware that she was capable of... glee.

"That's definitely for the best. Our species is often envied for its strength, but it comes at a great sacrifice." Her joyful expression dimmed as she stared at her feet. "If I could trade half my strength for another few years of life, I would do it in a heartbeat."

Danato regarded her slim-fitting outfit and decorated features. He hadn't really considered her age. Somewhere behind that makeup may have been the start of wrinkles, but that was hardly an indicator of her body's burden. Every change she endured took months off her potential lifespan. Even with the longevity that her pregnancies gave her, she wouldn't live past forty.

"I'm sure anyone would in your situation. But you said the hormone replacements have been working. Perhaps the lack of change will allow your species a longer lifespan than humans."

Leona tilted her head, examining him. "You are much more of an enigma than I ever gave you credit for."

"How's that?"

"You have a very contradictory personality. You despise my presence here. I sense it every time you look at me, and yet you have such compassion for my trials."

"I've watched too many werewolves die not to have compassion for the changes you endure. I wouldn't dare say that I pity you, but I do sympathize."

"I pity us," Leona said sardonically. "We are slaves to our hormones."

"Humans alike," Danato agreed.

"Yes, I suppose so. Would you mind if I sit?" She motioned to the chair in front of the desk.

Danato examined the chair. He mentally measured the distance between them, calculating her arm's reach, and the lack of exit options. He wondered at that moment if werewolf strength was any match against the entity's presence in his office. Since it wasn't an issue of strength so much as spacial redistribution, he doubted he had anything to fear from Leona.

He motioned for her to take the seat, and she did. She sighed as if she had been on her feet for hours. To his knowledge, she had been sitting in a helicopter most of the evening, followed by sitting in a meeting. He doubted their short tussle could have been responsible for her exhaustion.

Leona shifted her neck, rolling it over her shoulders. Her apparently aching body let out several cracks, followed by a zipper of cracks down her spine when she arched her back. She gave him a soft smile when she noticed his perplexed expression. "I didn't transform completely, but things got plenty out of whack."

"I see. I have some painkillers if you're interested." Danato pulled open his drawer, but Leona waved him away.

"Thank you, no. It's not wise to reduce the inflammation artificially. Besides, the pain will be gone in a few hours. I just need to *man up*, as they say."

Danato frowned at her. "You shouldn't have come so soon after your change."

"That wasn't entirely up to me. Actually, I think Cleos prefers to travel with me when I am weak. Despite his purported intellectual superiority, he is still just a man—and a feeble one at that."

Danato let out an unintentional snort at the insult. He was pleased Leona was immune to his charms. "How did you two meet?"

"He found me. It was at one of my sister's many functions. A gala of some kind—I don't even remember. She had so many of them. That was what being the high matriarch meant to her: parties, prestige, and pampering."

"And what does it mean to you?"

Leona caught the undertone of accusation in his voice and gave him a stony glare. "You have to give me some credit, Danato. I am making some legitimately useful changes."

"I'm no one to judge how you handle your people. I'm just a human."

"And yet you do. I've come all this way to offer an olive branch, and now you're smacking me in the face with it."

Danato shifted away from his desk, giving himself more room to defend himself if need be.

"Oh, for God's sake, Danato! I just came in here for a conversation!" Leona stood from her chair. "I have a toddler, an infant, and an endless stream of subjects crying to me all day long. I thought that, perhaps being the warden of this place, we might have a little common ground. I thought maybe we could... talk!" Leona pushed down her skirt and stormed out.

Danato sat flabbergasted behind his desk. Had it been any other woman—any human woman, he would have already been racing down the hall to apologize. However, had Leona been human, he wouldn't have treated her so standoffishly in the first place.

He glanced at the contract on his desk. He really needed to read it again, but he didn't want to. The burdens of being a monster were finally going to topple him in less than 24 hours. Either the world was going to end or his world was going to end. He wasn't angry or sad, like he should have been. He accepted his fate, and that terrified him more than anything.

Danato stood and rushed out the office door. He jogged down the hall and caught Leona grabbing the door to exit the building. Fortunately, she had stopped to put on a coat or he wouldn't have caught her.

"Leona," he called to her. She stopped and looked at him. For a moment, he didn't know what to say. "Do you want to have some coffee?" He motioned toward the cafeteria.

She paused and sniffed the air. She released the door and slipped off her coat. "Coffee sounds wonderful."

10

ETHAN ARRIVED ON THE seventh floor and took a moment to gaze at Duke's statue. He didn't dare move any closer to it. Every fiber of his being still wanted to rip him off that pedestal. Beyond his hero instincts, the cursed marble was calling to him like a siren of the sea. It was difficult to determine where his longing ended and the baiting thoughts began. If it weren't for the dire situation at hand, he might not be able to resist either influence.

Tearing himself away from his friend, he moved across the expansive space that was now under Cleos's purview. Cubicle lab spaces and supply storage occupied the center of the floor. Meanwhile, artifacts filled the aisles, each of them on display or barely contained. Ethan didn't consider this setup any safer than the prop room, but he no longer cared what happened to the junk. Least of all, that bloody lamp.

Ethan found Cleos meandering around one of the lab spaces, searching or perhaps exploring the drawers and cupboards. He now wore a bandage on his neck, making Ethan mildly curious about what transpired after he left the meeting.

Though Ethan had done nothing to silence his footsteps, his arrival made Cleos jump. After a moment to collect himself, his face shifted into the same expression he had seen earlier that morning on the roof. He had never known Cleos to be compassionate or even sympathetic, but he was certainly capable of pity.

And oh, how Ethan deserved pity.

Cleos braced his hands on the other side of the pristinely white countertop and lowered his gaze. For once, the man had nothing sarcastic or pompous to say.

"Did you know?" Ethan tossed out a soft question. They could work up to the harder questions.

"That you're a mage?" Cleos clarified, and Ethan nodded. "No. Although I'm not surprised, from what I understand about that level of magic, it has far less to do with the mind as it does the heart."

Ethan almost laughed at that. If his magic were in any way connected to his heart, the world would be on fire right now.

"Do you want to hear something strange?" Cleos asked as he continued to look around the space. "I can't hear the dragons."

Ethan nodded. "I'm not sure their minds work the same as ours."

"No, I mean in your memories." Cleos paused in his inventory to look at him. "I can't hear the words they thought to you. It's a one-sided conversation."

This didn't surprise Ethan in the least either, but he suspected it was a sore spot for Cleos. He was never fond of anyone he couldn't read like a book. "I take it that means you can't help me unlock my power?"

Cleos shook his head. "Magic is sloppy, but it has rules. I can't unlock what I can't see or feel." After a beat, he said, "However..." His mouth twisted in thought. "Should you wish to seek a greater understanding of what you are, I would suggest seeking out a powerful witch."

"Annette is dying."

Cleos dipped his brow. "No, I was thinking about someone higher. I would recommend Zara, but she's liable to eat you alive rather than help you. Rin *(REEN)* is fairly stable, but the Japanese underworld is no place for foreigners. There are a few witches of repute in New Orleans. You could try one of them."

Ethan moved to a cabinet that held more than a few body parts submerged in formaldehyde. As curious as he was about the merging of science and magic, he didn't have the luxury of a long discussion. "You know what we're facing."

Cleos didn't answer. When Ethan turned back, he saw the vacancy on Cleos's face as his gaze shifted downward again.

"You know how powerful he is. You know we can't fight a god."

Cleos snorted. "You can only fight for one," he muttered under his breath.

"We've exhausted our options for escape." Ethan could hear the rasp in his voice as he relived the late hours of last night, just after they realized the threat against them was twofold. Ethan placed his hands against the cabinet and stared at his reflection in the glass. He hated himself at this moment. He hated what he was about to ask. And yet what other choice did he have? "I need you to stop him before he kills my son."

Cleos didn't respond. Ethan turned and found him staring at him with the same pity on his face as before. Cleos turned his head first left then right, the movement nearly imperceptible.

"Did you hear me!" Ethan yelled at him. "He is going to kill my son!"

"I know... and I'm sorry."

"Don't you tell me you're sorry!" Ethan moved back to the counter and sent what was probably a very expensive device crashing to the floor. "Don't you stand there with your purported superiority and tell me you can't do this for us—for her! I know you are capable of this... and so much more."

Cleos's eyes shut for a moment, and his lids fluttered. When he opened them again, his pity was but a memory. "I'm not saying I can't do it. I'm saying I won't do it."

Ethan stared at him, the shock of his refusal prickling up his spine along with a fresh wave of panic. He had never considered that Cleos would outright refuse his request. Certainly, he had expected him to have conditions for his participation, but never once had he imagined the man would do nothing to help them. "Are you really going to stand there and do nothing while my son is murdered?"

"Being the hero is not my job."

"And yet you've done it before."

"Circumstances that ultimately didn't affect me negatively."

Ethan narrowed his eyes and looked around the lab. "This?" He motioned to the floor. "You don't want to piss off Danato because you might lose your tenancy. Is that what you're weighing against the life of my child?"

"I don't doubt this is an excruciating moment for the two of you. But regardless of the loss of your son, the world will continue to turn. The sun will rise and set. However, if a genie *is risen* like the fucking antichrist, there is no guarantee that the cosmos will be running on schedule."

"We don't know what will happen."

"Exactly. But we do know what happens if your son dies. Danato has no choice but to make the play with the lowest risk." Cleos clenched his jaw and took a deep breath. "And support him."

Ethan stared at Cleos's hardened expression for a long time—searching for any sign of guilt or regret, but there was nothing beyond his resolution to back Danato's actions. He moved around the counter and stood near enough for Cleos to hear him whisper. "I know what happens if my son dies. Do you?" He moved to walk away.

"Ethan," Cleos said softly, drawing his attention back to him. "I understand that you and I are never going to be friends. I'm not really a buddy-buddy person, anyway. However, I think there is potential for an understanding between us. I understand that at any moment you could sneak up behind me and snap my neck like a twig. And I hope you understand it would only take a single touch for me to reduce you to a whimpering puppy dog at my feet." Cleos's eyes glinted with an almost carnivorous glee.

As frightened as Ethan should have been by this prospect, he was seeing Cleos differently than he had before. Though powerful, he was completely alone. "Is this place all you had?"

"What?"

"Is that why you're back here? Because you had nowhere else to go?"

Cleos chuckled.

"No one to go to?"

Cleos's amusement died almost instantly, but he quickly recovered his sarcasm. "Indeed. I've missed you all so terribly. That's why I've spent so much time and energy trying to save this dying industry. So, we can all gather together in this miserable excuse for a climate and wait for the next apocalypse."

"Why did you do all that? Why did a man with no loyalties bind himself to this place?"

The energy seemed to drain from Cleos as he shook his head. "That's a conversation for another awful day, Ethan. One I don't wish to hasten. Go be with your wife, Ethan."

Ethan nodded, but he had no intention of going to Cori. As much as they needed each other in this moment, their only recourse was to weep. But it was too soon to cry. There was still time to save his son. Cleos may not have been willing to help him, but there was still one man in this prison more powerful than Danato. The only question was whether their friendship was strong enough to ask him to commit murder.

11

DANATO POURED WHAT HAD to be his sixth cup of coffee since last night. He hadn't bothered going to bed after he had found out about the genie. No one had. He knew that his lack of sleep wouldn't make his mind any sharper, but he wasn't particularly hopeful that he would find a solution to the problem, so it was mostly guilt that was keeping him going at this point.

Danato poured a second cup and brought it to Leona, who had taken a seat at one of the tables. He was thankful that it was too early for breakfast. He wasn't exactly sure he wanted the staff gossiping about him having coffee with a fem-wolf.

"I'm sorry if I'm not being hospitable." Danato handed her the cup, which she immediately took a sip of. Her brow perked with approval, and she took another sip. "I'm not used to socializing with fem-wolves. And you don't exactly have the best reputation here."

"I can imagine. Cleos and I are quite a pair. I agree that he does not always put his best foot forward. And me—well, let's just say ego is something one doesn't always grow out of." Leona winked at him.

He allowed a small smile for her effort to amuse him. "What do you want, Leona?"

"I want what Cleos wants. I want to—"

"From me?" Danato clarified. "You and I have never chatted. Why now? Are you hoping to manipulate me? Because you should really reconsider my experience before you attempt that."

Leona stared at him, mouth agape and slightly taken aback by his accusation. She looked at her coffee and set it down on the table. "I used to delight in seeing powerful men cower before me—especially human men. Suffice it to say, it is an aphrodisiac that many fem-wolves have a taste for." Danato's tolerance of their conversation faded, but he didn't interrupt her. "It takes most men several encounters to truly feel the level of fear that they should. To understand that I am not just 'strong for a girl' or stronger than a man, but that I am the strongest."

Danato allowed himself to relax when he realized this wasn't a conversation about lust so much as pride. "You said you used to delight in that."

"Oui. The appeal fades with time—with age, I think." Leona tapped her mug. "I know you and I are not friends, but you are different."

"Different?"

"You are *between*." Leona knit her fingers together. "The first time I visited, you seemed so..."

"If you say docile, I'm going to have to leave." Danato offered her a small smile to let her know he was mostly joking.

Leona threw her head back and laughed. "No, I don't think that word could have ever described you. I smelled your fear, but what was most impressive was your composure. Today was the first time I saw you lose that composure."

"I don't enjoy showing my temper like that. It's unnecessary and boorish. But sometimes it's the only way to get anyone's attention."

Leona smiled. "I know how you feel. Being a werewolf and looking like this—" She motioned to her body, no doubt meaning to emphasize her petite frame. "—doesn't exactly inspire fear. Except in those who are smart enough to understand that size doesn't equate to ability."

"I imagine it doesn't take you too long to educate them."

Leona's eyes dipped as if she were embarrassed by the topic. "Let's just say I've broken a few hands that have landed on my rear end in error."

Danato chuckled, imagining the surprised looks on the faces of the men who dared to take liberties with a werewolf. "I'm sure they deserved it."

"I suppose I should be grateful. If I were a mere human, I would only have my voice and wit to defend against the will of others. Sometimes I try to imagine what it must be like for other women. To know that at any moment a male of even equal stature could easily hurt you. It's no wonder they pair up so readily with a mate." Leona's eyes glazed over for a moment. "I myself don't require such constant attention."

Danato didn't respond, but he wondered if that were true. He knew that werewolves rarely paired up—at least not for long, but was it truly because the females desired autonomy? Or was this yet another cultural demand claimed as natural instinct?

"I have suitors certainly," Leona added, lest Danato think men found her undesirable. "But they aren't exactly there for conversation."

She was flaunting now. Danato despised bragging. It was the lowest form of conversing—the equivalent of a dog begging for scraps from a dinner. However, it was especially detestable coming from a werewolf. A creature that was effectively at the top of the food chain.

"I suppose that makes me sound like a whore to you."

Danato frowned at her accusation. "Of course not."

"Don't human males prefer women to be virtuous and submissive?"

Danato's lip twitched as he contemplated how to respond. "I have no expectations for the entirety of the female population, certainly not fem-wolves. Not that my opinion should matter in the least to you."

Leona stared at him—an odd sort of sadness on her face. "Even if I did want to talk, there is no one who would understand." She took a sip of her coffee, letting the cup linger at the edge of her lip long after she had swallowed. "No one ever talks about it, do they?"

"What's that?"

"The burden of superiority." Leona's eyes flashed at him. "And I don't just mean the strength. I mean a position of power—being the one that everyone turns to for the answers." Danato looked up at the two guards who entered the cafeteria. They gave him the usual nods, but when their gazes lingered a little too long on Leona's low-cut top and short skirt, he cleared his throat. They noted his disapproval and moved on.

"I thought being the leader of my people would be easy." Leona continued. "I thought I would take the reins and everything would go smoothly because I was in control."

"Not very smooth, I take it?"

Leona scoffed and took a breath. "Oh, Danato, I'm surrounded by morons." Danato snorted, unable to contain his amusement. He couldn't claim that his staff were morons, but they did require some babysitting. He could at the very least empathize with that. "Sometimes I feel like I am just a sounding board for other people's problems. Nearly everyone is angry with my decisions, and those that aren't are trying to take advantage of me. I feel like I worked my whole life just to become a title."

Danato stared back at her, understanding everything she was saying as if it had come from his own mouth. He remembered a time when he ranted the same complaints to Belus. "You're new to power. Eventually, you'll forget who you used to be. Then it won't bother you so much that you lost her."

Leona frowned and looked down at the table. "I wouldn't mind it so much, but it means that my children will lose her too."

Danato nodded in understanding—though he couldn't possibly know anything about that burden. Taking charge of the prison hadn't cost him nearly that much. Certainly, if he had been older, he would have had a family to consider, but his thoughts of marriage and children came much later and much too late.

"That must be difficult for you," he said, trying to sound sympathetic even though he was questioning why Leona was being so open with him. His contact with the fem-wolf had been limited to two visits to the prison, both of which she spent as much time irritating his successors as possible. Their brief interactions had only given him enough time to conclude that, like most werewolves, she was an arrogant, domineering narcissist, who preferred to posture rather than communicate.

This sudden change in her character was making Danato leery of her motives. It was usually Cori or Ethan that she attempted to manipulate. Why this sudden interest in him? Had Cleos brought her here for a purpose beyond his purported agenda?

Leona's gaze danced over him—no doubt reading him like a book. Her sense of smell was diminished compared to Nevia's, but she could certainly smell the distrust on him. "I didn't mean to throw my troubles at your feet. I just thought that you might understand." Leona slumped back in her chair. With the tension in her spine released, her body sagged down, making her look every bit the part of the fragile damsel in distress. She needed only cry, and Danato would be helpless against his chivalrous instincts.

He still didn't trust her, but he knew her statements were true, and he couldn't resist reaching out to the common thread they shared—a common burden. He, like she, had power over a great number of people. People who respected or hated or loved him—occasionally all at once. "I do understand, Leona." Her head popped up, and her face revealed a relief he hadn't expected. "I'm more than happy to commiserate with you on the topic of leadership, but..."

Leona took a breath and stiffened her back as if she already knew what this speech might entail.

"You have a history here. One that makes me reluctant to trust your candor."

"You think I'm manipulating you?"

"I think you're a smart woman, Leona, and you know how to get people to do what you want."

"You forgot sexy. Smart *and* sexy."

Danato stared at her with a blank expression. "I don't really think of you in those terms."

Leona's brow dipped as she examined him. "You really don't, do you?" she asked introspectively. "I could be sitting here in sweatpants or a bikini and you would not treat me any differently."

Danato cleared his throat—disappointed that she was, once again, focusing on herself rather than what he was saying. "This is not about fashion, Leona. This is about teamwork. If Cleos really wants to bring werewolves into this facility as hunters—then you will need to be an example for them. I can't have you playing your games."

"What games?"

Danato clenched his jaw. He had no room to show anger, but he felt it nonetheless. "I am aware of the interactions that you've had with Cori and Ethan."

"Oh, that," she said dismissively.

"Yes, that."

"That was a lifetime ago. So much has changed since then."

"Perhaps, but personalities don't change as quickly as circumstances."

"I admit, there is something about Cori that puts my cackles up, but I have no intention of harming her."

"Good, because much like I told Cleos. There is no place here for anyone who doesn't respect my crew."

Leona's lip tipped up, and she reached across the table. Danato moved to retract his hands but stopped himself. She rested her hand over his and stroked her thumb once over his fingers. "It's sweet how protective you are of her." Danato glared at her—taking her statement as mocking. She rolled her eyes and leaned in a little more. "Danato,

I promise you. I have no desire to hurt Cori. My candor is in earnest." She drew away from him and pinched her lips before speaking. "However, it is ill-timed. You have much more pressing matters to deal with than listening to an aging fem-wolf complain about her job." Leona stood from the table and pushed her chair back into place. "Strength and power don't mean as much in these situations, do they?" Danato shook his head. "Do you have any defense worth pursuing?"

"Defense? No."

"Perhaps you will yet find something in the texts."

Danato nodded in agreement. That's what he had been saying all night as he read and reread the same three pages over and over again. The truth was, there was nothing in the handbook about corporealization. This was not a preset condition of the genie lamp that could be researched. This was a private agreement. A contract signed in blood while blindfolded, but nonetheless, it was a valid accord. And there was nothing Danato could do to break it. Nothing except...

"Danato, if you would need... I mean if the time would come and—"

"You should get some rest." Danato stood abruptly. "I'm sure you didn't get any sleep on the way here."

Leona looked him over, wearing a sympathetic gaze that bordered on pity. "Je suis désolé que ton fardeau soit trop lourd," she whispered before leaving the cafeteria.

Danato stared after her, mulling over the same sentence that had clouded his mind for hours. *The child must be of warm flesh and no name to receive the energy of the universe.*

It was the only portion of the documents that even remotely related to their situation, and yet, it offered no other details. No loopholes, no clauses, not even conditions that would allow this contract to be made to begin with. It was simply an instruction manual for the transference of the cosmos from one form to another. It was as if someone had slipped a recipe right smack dab in the middle of the Bible. It didn't make sense for it to be there—nor was it even a complete recipe. It was just ingredients and rules about eating said recipe after it was complete. In the end, it was useless—except that it confirmed what Danato had feared. He was once again going to have to prevent a human from gaining a power that was well beyond the natural limitations of witchcraft.

12

CORI HAD BEEN POURING over books and contracts with Belus almost nonstop since she had first heard about the genie's threat. They had been up all night. Cleos's arrival in the wee hours of the morning couldn't have come at a worse time. The fact that he brought two of her least favorite people with him was like a kick in the face and a stab in the back at the same time. She knew her anger had more to do with the threat against her child, but she still resented him for coming back.

Why now?

Of all the times in her life, why did he have to find her at her lowest?

Cori erupted into tears. It wasn't the first time, and it wouldn't be the last. She put her face in her hands trying to spare the documents beneath her a shower. "I need you to say it," she blubbered into her palms.

She heard Belus shift to put down his cup of coffee. When she looked up, he was staring at her from his chair. She had opted to work at his house because she needed her mentor now more than ever. She needed his mind. His years of experience. Most of all, she needed his honesty.

"Just say it," she pleaded again.

Belus didn't move. His stoic facade didn't waver, even though she was certain he knew what she was asking. They had talked and talked in circles, going over the incident, and redefining the parameters of the contract. Danato and Belus had explained the dangers of a universal power aligning with a human form. Power, magic, consequences, risks. They had danced verbally, but no one, not even Belus had ever said the words. Even though they were all thinking it.

"Tell me what happens if we don't find a solution in time." Cori felt herself tremble as Belus opened his mouth to speak.

"We just have to keep looking, Cori."

Cori threw her book down, rattling the glass on the coffee table. "I already know the answer."

"Then you don't need me to say it."

"I do need you to say it. I need to hear the words that my mind keeps repeating over and over again. I have to let them out."

Belus turned to look at the door before speaking. "You won't let me coddle you and shield you, just this once?" he asked.

Cori chuffed and shrugged. "Let's give it a try. Tell me everything is going to be okay."

"Everything will be okay," Belus said, playing along.

Cori felt her tears bloom again. "Tell me this is all just a misunderstanding."

He paused, swallowing hard before speaking the words she was asking for. "It's all just a misunderstanding."

"Tell me my baby boy is going to live a long and happy life with Papa Danato and Uncle Belus."

He finally broke, his face constricting in agonizing grief. His eyes watered, and he turned his head to look away from her. His jaw tensed as he tried to struggle through the emotions that were overwhelming him. Belus had a strong heart, but even he loved that child. Even he would be torn apart by his absence in their lives.

"He will live," Belus said through the duress of encroaching tears. "We will find a way." Belus gritted his teeth, cleared his throat, and went back to his books.

Cori waited nearly a minute before speaking. "And if we don't?" She asked quietly with no particular emotion backing it.

Belus didn't look up, but she saw him taking a deep, slow inhalation. After a beat, he finally answered. "Then he must die."

Cori felt the words hit her like an icy adrenaline shock. It coursed through her veins, making her hands and feet go instantly cold. As tethered as her heart was to her child, she felt something snap in that moment. She was certain it was just reality catching up with her. She lived in a world that offered adventure and excitement, but it also provided danger and pain.

When she considered the numbness in her mind a moment longer, she realized what had broken. The connection between her heart and mind. She finally felt what it must have been like for Danato to choose to kill his own wife. To make a decision for the benefit of the prison and the world instead of himself. It was a hopeless feeling, but it was also weightless. As if she had just died in that moment, and only needed to go through the motions of the remainder of her life as a ghost.

She looked down at the documents on the table and picked them up. She wasn't really reading them. She was just staring at them. The words that filled the pages no longer mattered. Nothing mattered now.

13

Danato arrived home to what he thought would be an empty house. Cori and Ethan, intentionally or otherwise, had been keeping their distance from him. He was, after all, their child's judge and jury—and possibly his executioner. The possibility of murdering a child had never in all his life occurred to him. To take the life of someone so young—so innocent, made no sense to him. Knowing that a genie—a being with unfathomable knowledge of humanity—could be so cruel, made his body prickle with the physical heat of rage. But there was nothing he could do to diminish that anger.

Danato noticed someone sitting in his usual chair and narrowed his eyes to focus on whoever was dimly lit by the dying fire in the hearth. "What the hell are you doing in my house?" he asked when he recognized Gypsy's slumped form.

The fire found new life and brought a warm glow to the woman's black-on-black ensemble. She took a breath and sat up. She looked around as if confused about her location. She caught sight of Danato and groaned. "Damn it. I fell asleep."

"Fell asleep or passed out?" Danato came over to her and ripped the half-empty vodka bottle from her sleepy grasp. Gypsy didn't answer or apologize for the theft of his fine liquor. He recapped the bottle and put it back in the so-called hidden compartment behind the wainscoting. "What are you doing here besides stealing my liquor?"

"I had to have a talk with Efrat in private."

"Efrat?" Danato looked around for signs of damage on his furniture or walls. "And why couldn't you have it in the prison?"

"The walls have ears." Gypsy slurred and held her hand to her ear. Her body rocked slightly as her hooded eyes tried to study him.

"You're drunk, Gypsy," he declared as if she might not have known.

"It's the altitude." She chuckled and dropped her head against him.

Danato rolled his eyes and pushed her away by the shoulders. "Why are you drunk?"

Gypsy pointed to his now hidden stash of liquor. He shook his head. "No, I don't mean *how* are you drunk. I mean, why?"

"Why not?" She shrugged as best she could while still being held in his grip.

"I'm not going to claim to know you well enough to predict your proclivities, Grace, but I know that you aren't the type to fall asleep on the job. That would make you vulnerable to attack. And you are never unprepared for an attack." Danato released her and propped his hands on his hips. "So, I'll ask you again. Why are you drunk?"

Gypsy's eyes widened or at least fully opened. Her face was a mixture of emotions that he couldn't pinpoint. She was either angry or upset, but since he wasn't expecting the woman to erupt into tears, he tensed for an attack.

And attack she did.

Gypsy lunged at him, wrapping her arms around his neck like a python ready to strangle him—albeit from the wrong side. He shifted back to allow himself the room to toss her onto the couch should she refuse to release him.

The headbutt he anticipated never came. Instead, Gypsy's lips mashed into his. Shocked by the aggressive intimacy, he tried to back away further, but she was hanging from his neck and nothing short of brute strength would remove her.

When he felt her tongue force its way between his lips, his stomach lurched with disgust. Younger women may tempt some men, but Danato preferred women of equal maturity—and Grace Gypsum was far from mature in his eyes. Not to mention, she was a psychopath.

Danato wrenched her arms off his neck and pushed her away. He took a necessary breath as he held her wrists captive behind her so she couldn't *attack* again. "Stop this!"

"Come on, Danato. We have the house to ourselves."

"Gypsy, this game is never going to work on me! Do you understand me?"

"It never did." Gypsy shifted, trying to remove herself from his grip, which was keeping them uncomfortably close. "Let me go," she demanded.

"Are you going to behave?"

"Not by a long shot. Maybe you should punish me," she said seductively and bit her lip.

"Is that your only defense against me?" Danato shifted forward and pushed her back into his chair. She flopped down into the comfy chair and glared at him. She tried to get up again, and he pushed her down. She gave him another glare and tried to kick him in the face. He grabbed her foot and shoved it away just as the other foot tried to wrack him. Several attempts to punch him also went unanswered as he batted her away like a fly. He thought she might have had better luck against him sober, but at this moment, he was stronger, faster, and not in the least afraid of her.

After she spent all her energy, leaving her panting and sweating, she gnashed her teeth together. "I will kill you."

The words shouldn't have had any effect on him. It wasn't the first time someone had threatened to murder him. It wasn't even the first time a woman had. However, the coolness in her eyes told him it wasn't just a warning. She was simply stating her intentions.

Had it been any other woman or a prisoner saying it, he would have just walked away with no fear of retaliation. However, he remembered what Nevia had said about Gypsy being like fire. Helpful if used correctly, but devastating if not monitored carefully.

Danato was used to brandishing his strength to get what he wanted from most people, but Gypsy was not *most* people. Challenging her would only result in a deep-seated hatred that over time would fester and backfire at the worst possible time. He needed to handle her differently.

"I guess that means we won't be making out anymore." Danato took a step back. "Get up." Gypsy narrowed her eyes at the command. "Stand up." He motioned her up with a finger.

She moved slowly, and he monitored her hands to make sure she had no intention of pulling one of her many hidden weapons. When they were back in a standoff position, he motioned her out of the living room and placed his hand very lightly against her back.

Gypsy moved forward, shifting her head to keep him in her peripheral vision. She tried to angle toward the front door, but he shifted into her path and once again motioned her onward. When they reached the kitchen island, he pulled out one of the stools. "Sit," he said and moved around the counter.

Gypsy stood next to the stool and watched him move about the kitchen. He turned on the stove burners and put his favorite cast-iron skillet on the heat. He walked to the fridge and pulled out eggs, milk, and bacon. Then he grabbed a box of pancake mix and coffee from the pantry cupboard. "How do you take your eggs?" he asked when she still hadn't sat down.

She scoffed and crossed her arms. "Are you serious?"

"I'm always serious about eggs." Danato started a pot of coffee while the skillet warmed up.

"Why are you cooking me breakfast?"

"Because it's too late for supper and too damn early for lunch. No better remedy for a night of drinking than bacon and eggs." Danato propped his hands on the counter. "You strike me as an omelet kind of girl."

Gypsy leaned on the other side of the counter, mirroring his position. "This game won't work on me either. Do you think the cockles of my heart will be warmed by your tender father-figure persona?"

Danato grimaced and shook his head. "Perhaps we should skip the references to my fatherly mystique while I still have the taste of your tongue in my mouth."

Gypsy snorted but contained her laughter. When she still didn't sit down, he returned to the stove and started placing bacon on the skillet. The sizzling meat instantly released the aroma of breakfast and made his mouth water. "The door is open, Gypsy. You're welcome to get your breakfast in the cafeteria. The powdered eggs aren't as tasty as mine, but they fill a belly just fine."

She finally sat down, surrendering perhaps not to him, but to the smell of bacon and coffee. Few could resist that peace offering. He continued preparing the meal in silence. Gypsy stood at one point to pour herself a cup of coffee. She poured him one as well and handed it off to him between flipped pancakes.

Somewhere between his bacon crisping to perfection and the last pancake flipping, she spoke. "She blames me for the child being in danger."

Danato turned and looked at her. He would have given anything to have Nevia sitting next to the woman at that moment. He wanted to know what emotion had been extorted by Cori's accusation.

"I would never harm a child." Gypsy hadn't raised her voice, but a deep, urgent tone forced the words from her mouth. She seemed to be defending herself to him.

"I believe you." And he did. He didn't trust her, but he could rely on her not to mince words or sweet-talk him. She had no reason to lie, because she didn't care what anyone thought of her truth.

Danato grabbed a plate from the cupboard and loaded up bacon, eggs, and an unhealthy portion of pancakes for her. He placed the plate before her and pushed the syrup and butter over before making a plate for himself.

"Did you ever get the rundown on how Cori and Ethan arrived here?" he asked, wondering how translucent Cleos had been with Gypsy. Though he could have given Gypsy every single memory he had ever observed from Cori, he knew he wouldn't. Placing too many disconnected memories into the wrong mind was dangerous. Personalities change; sometimes they even mirror the subject of the memories. If Cleos had given

Gypsy Cori's life story, then she might have developed a split personality.

Since Gypsy already had a full bite of food, she wobbled her hand, signifying that she had some of the story. Danato took a bite of bacon, unable to resist appeasing his appetite a little before conversing further.

"Cori was held in captivity for two weeks before I purchased her. I don't think I have to explain what happens to women who are destined for a life of slavery." Gypsy shook her head. "Cleos claims to have rid her of most of the lucid memories of those events. He left her just enough to keep her bruised, but not broken. And of course, her relationship with Ethan and me helped her feel safe here." Danato chuckled, thinking about the incident with Dirk. It wasn't the most ideal outcome, but only because he would have preferred to make an example of the man himself. "She defends herself pretty well too, though."

"What does this have to do with me?" Gypsy asked, more inquisitive than annoyed, though he was certain she wasn't in the mood to hear him talk wistfully about his team.

"As I've interpreted Cori's retelling of her altered timeline, you seemed to end up having a similar fate before coming to the prison to work for me." Danato paused to let her take that in, but she seemed more interested in lapping up the syrup with her pancakes. "I don't doubt you have a very specific moral code that you live by, Gypsy, but there is no telling what trauma like that would do to an already damaged mind."

"Damaged mind," Gypsy mumbled over the pancake. She took a sip of coffee and cleared her throat. "What do you think I am, Danato? A stroke victim?"

"I know Cori blames you for what's happening, but we can no more blame you for this than a kicked dog for biting someone."

Gypsy stared at him. The amusement lurking in her eyes looked remarkably like pity. "What are you going to do? To save the child, I mean."

Danato rubbed his face and turned his attention to his food. "There is very little we can do."

"But if a genie becomes human, he'll be free from his confines. He could... I don't know, but it's bad, right?"

"Yes, it's bad, but we won't allow it to go that far."

Gypsy regarded him coolly, not surrendering her grip on his eyes. "You're going to execute him, aren't you? Just like you did that sorceress?"

Danato cringed and shook his head. "I've discussed a less traumatizing procedure with the doctor. Something more akin to putting an animal to sleep."

"Goddammit, Danato, don't give in like that. If I could stop those wizards with a fucking fork, then surely somebody can—what about Daniel?" Danato looked up at her confused. "His power is deep, dark, and deadly. If anyone can topple that Arabian piece of shit, it's him, right? Let's cock the Irish bastard and get this over with."

Danato wondered if that were true. Would Daniel have had enough power to destroy a being of such magnitude? Or would they cancel each other out? He didn't know enough about either to predict, but he would have been willing to try. If he were still alive.

"I'm sorry, Gypsy," Danato said quietly. "I just assumed someone had told you."

"Told me what?"

"Daniel was stabbed to death yesterday." Gypsy froze and stared at him. "A rogue transmorph did it. She was also killed. Nevia went missing after the incident and may be feral. Heaton and Callin went after her against my wishes. I haven't even had a chance to deal with that offense."

Gypsy's eyes sank down to her plate. "I didn't think he could be killed. How can someone with that much power just... die?"

"Every man can die."

Gypsy's mouth opened, and her head tipped back as if something had just occurred to her. "No wonder everyone is giving up."

"We aren't giving up, Gypsy. You've just arrived at the end of a very long day, and the beginning of what we anticipate to be the worst day of our lives. I welcome your ideas, but what you must understand is that I will eventually have to make a choice. Risk the fate of the world or kill a child that I consider my grandson. And since I know what the answer is, I have to prepare myself for that outcome."

Gypsy nodded and stood up. "I get it. I really do. Block off the emotions so you can think clearly and make wise choices. Consider the consequences and avoid the greater risks in the long run." She wiped her face and yanked her high ponytail a little tighter. "That's not how I work, though. If you think for one second that you can save the day by questioning your choices three steps ahead of yourself, you're wrong. You just jump in and fix the rest of the problems as they arise." She headed to the door.

"Easy to say with a fork in your back pocket."

Gypsy paused at the door and looked back at him.

"It won't work," he cautioned before her plots could solidify. "A genie is more powerful than time itself. He won't allow you to use the fork to rewrite the day. It would take far more magical influence than spellbound flatware to save the child."

Her eyes narrowed slightly. "There you go again. Thinking about the consequences when you should be acting."

Danato nodded somberly. "I won't stop you, Gypsy. I would gladly be in your debt for saving the world again. But I will caution you. When the time runs out. I will do my duty."

Gypsy pinched her lips and ripped open the door. She stopped in the frame and looked back at him. "And I will not stand by and watch you murder an innocent child."

Danato pinned her with a hollow gaze. "Then close your eyes."

Gypsy snarled and slammed the door. Danato leaned over the counter, feeling the day falling in around him. Sorrow demons were already nipping at his ankles, more than ready to climb on for another long meal. His mask fell away, and his breath became stuttered. Long overdue tears dripped onto his breakfast as his quiet rasping exhales shook his mammoth shoulders.

14

GYPSY COULDN'T REMEMBER BEING angrier than she was at that moment. She understood that the weight of the world was pressing everyone down. Perhaps if Duke weren't stuck in a statue and if Daniel weren't flat on a slab, they could all focus on something other than the pain. As it stood now, the entire prison seemed to be preparing for an inevitable fate.

Well, she sure as hell wasn't.

Gypsy had only a few rules in her messed-up little brain. And number one was that children were off limits. She didn't kill kids, not even if they tried to kill her. A good whack on the ass to straighten them up, maybe, but that was it.

As soon as the doors of the elevator opened on the top floor, Gypsy tore through the room in search of the man who was really responsible for all this bullshit. She passed up more than a few potential weapons and freaky-looking masks before she hit the pedestal that held an unpolished brass oil lamp.

Gypsy lifted it, freely touching its font. When nothing happened, she banged the damn thing on the white-painted wood beneath it. "Get out here, you motherfucker!"

"You shouldn't be playing with things you can't understand." A deep voice spoke behind her. Gypsy whipped around and saw a bald, bronzed-skinned badass behind her.

"You the genie?" she asked, though by the looks of the slightly undulating black tattoos on his skin, he wasn't quite human. The genie looked down at the shifting artwork on his forearm and rubbed his hand over it.

"Who are you?" he asked.

"I want my three wishes," Gypsy demanded.

The genie tilted his head, inspecting her. "Is that so?"

"Yes. Here it goes. I wish you were dead." Gypsy took a step closer to him with each wish. "I wish you were dead. And oh, I wish you were dead."

On the final wish, they were face to face, practically ready to kiss. The light around him flared. She felt the warmth of it, and somewhere deep inside she could feel a tug of authority, but she ignored it. If she was immune to the overflow of emotions coming off a dark-magic-infused sorceress, she wasn't sure this guy had any chance of impressing her with a lame-ass light show. To guarantee that he understood how unimpressed she was, she spat in his face.

The genie wiped away her dribble and smiled at her. "Who is this enchantress before me?" he asked again, wariness bleeding into his voice.

"Grace Gypsum, otherwise known as—"

"Gypsy," the genie finished for her, delight illuminating his features. "I should thank you."

"Thank me for what?"

"You are the reason that my hope of being in an earthly body has come true."

"No, that little dream of yours was constructed by you and you alone."

"It was your blade that necessitated it. If not for that, I would have simply disappeared, never to return."

"You want to blame this on me, go ahead."

"I think I just did."

"Fine, then punish me."

The genie's form disappeared and reappeared farther away from her. "I have no desire or reason to harm you."

"If I am the reason for the debt, then I should pay the price."

"The debt has already been paid, and the pact has already been signed. There is no going back on it now. I have a body to reside in. I will not waver."

"Take my body, not the child's!" Gypsy pounded her chest. "What do you want with a little kid? I've got everything you could possibly need right here." She extended her arms to display her potential.

The genie shook his head slowly. "That offer has already been made by more than one. As I said to all of them, I will say to you, there is no pact between us. My accord is with the boy."

"How can you have an accord with a baby? He wasn't even born when you made this deal."

"Time is irrelevant to me. I exist eternally and ubiquitously."

"I don't even know what the hell that means, but you are not possessing the child if I have anything to say about it."

The genie perked his eyebrow at her. "It would seem that you have plenty to say about it, but it will do you no good to pander or preach to me. The laws of men do not control me." The genie raised his arm, showing off his tattoos. "These are the only rules that influence me."

Gypsy cracked her neck and moved forward. "Well then, let's get a magic fucking marker and change some of the rules." Before the genie could weasel away from her, she planted a nose-cracking punch on him. Or it would have been if he hadn't phased out just in time.

Her fist split the smoketrail he left behind. She sensed him behind her and repositioned for a roundhouse kick. Her boot heel narrowly missed his fading chin.

With only a heartbeat between, she threw another punch at the belly before her, and a jump spin to the chest at her back. Each time, the smoky air trailed behind her efforts. Soon she was surrounded by only smoke and no genie. She stopped moving and waited, sucking in the air while she could.

A moment later, the genie appeared everywhere around her. His multiple bodies circled her, taunting her with power she did not possess. At least not without half a dozen bone swords.

"Must I display my power so that you can understand?" the genie asked.

Gypsy nodded and circled to look at them all. "I'm a slow learner. I think you're going to have to teach me a harder lesson."

"As you wish." The genie and his replicates disappeared.

"Oh, now you're taking wishes!" Gypsy raised her arms in frustration.

"Touch me if you dare," his voice whispered behind her. She turned and saw that he was fully tangible—no wisps of smoke, no blurred edges.

Gypsy turned to face him, checking him for weapons—not because he needed any, but just out of habit. Rather than bother with a punch or kick, Gypsy raised her finger, brandishing a slightly long nail, and pointed it at him threateningly. She moved it forward dramatically, showing her lack of deference to his grandeur.

When her finger hit his chest, something in his eyes changed. He looked down at the connection with shock. Her amusement with his lackluster power waned when a familiar and unwelcome feeling came over her. Only this time the flood of emotions—pain, joy, hate, and love—came with memories.

Memories that didn't belong to her.

Gypsy screamed in agony as five thousand years of pain bubbled to the surface of her mind, tearing at her sanity like nails on a chalkboard. She dropped to the floor and curled into a ball, all the while trying to claw the emotions out of her mind.

By the time she realized Cleos had arrived to subdue her, she had put deep rents into her forehead and scalp. There was blood all over her hands, and it was dripping into her eyes. She turned and saw that it was smearing onto Cleos's suit.

"Your suit," she mumbled.

Cleos shushed her gently, petting her hair back. She usually didn't let him touch her—for obvious reasons and trust issues—but at that moment he was a life preserver to her. "Never mind all that. Let's get you to the infirmary."

He pushed her away from his chest and stood. He reached down and yanked her upward by the hand. She looked back at the genie, who was still standing there examining her.

"What are you?" he asked, now officially irritated with her.

"What the fuck are you?" she asked.

"Don't interact with him," Cleos scolded, yanking on her tethered hand again.

"I am the power of the universe. The sun, the moon, the stars, and all the worlds among them."

"What did you just do to me?" Gypsy asked, not willing to leave without an answer.

"I didn't do anything. That was you." The genie tilted his head to one side and narrowed his eyes. "So, I ask you again... What are you?"

Gypsy felt a shiver up her spine as she backed away from the genie. She didn't understand crap about fairies, magic, and unicorns, but she knew when it was time to walk away from a fight.

15

"WHAT POSSESSED YOU TO take on a genie?" Cleos scolded as they stood in the elevator on the way down to the infirmary. She wasn't one for making a fuss over a few scratches, but she was still bleeding, and disinfectant was always a good thing.

"Is there some reason we are still holding hands?" Gypsy nodded down at their interlaced fingers. She had long since released her grip on him, but his claw-like fingernails were still pinching against her skin—ready to draw more blood. "You know I hate it when you touch me."

Cleos all but threw her hand back at her. "I should punish you for such stupidity." He pulled a pair of octagon sunglasses from the top pocket of his suit jacket and unfolded them.

Gypsy scoffed. "Please, after that episode, there is nothing you can do to shake me."

Cleos gave her a haughty glare before hiding his eyes behind a style that exacerbated his vampiric appearance. He didn't like her insolence, but despite his ire, he wouldn't do anything to her. Not because he couldn't. She knew it would only take a single thread of memories for him to crash her hard drive and bring her to her knees. He wouldn't do it because he needed her exactly as she was. She was, after all, a delicate balance of pain in the ass and usefulness.

"What did you feel?" he asked.

"It wasn't so much a feeling as a big dose of memories."

"Whose memories?" Cleos reached for her hand again, as if he had missed something on his initial read, but she pulled her hand away.

"His memories."

"The genie's?" Cleos reached again, but this time he didn't take no for an answer. He gripped her hand, and his eyes fluttered. She rolled her eyes and groaned. So much of her life was on display to him already, she wished he could back off once in a while. "I don't see anything," he said and released her hand.

"I would hope to hell not. It wasn't exactly something I wanted to hang on to." As it was, the only thing she could remember on her own was the image of being strapped down to a stone altar and pain. More pain than she could even comprehend.

The doors to the elevator opened, and Cori was on the other side with her little boy. They were walking by, hand in hand, and looked up when the doors opened. She immediately frowned at Cleos and turned the displeasure on her. Her irritation fluctuated as she took in Gypsy's appearance. In addition to the black eye that she had given her, Gypsy now looked like she had lost a fight with a rabid house cat.

"What happened to you?" she asked.

Gypsy stepped out and shrugged. "Turns out genies aren't to be messed with."

Cori's brow furrowed. Her son tugged on her hand, demanding that they keep going wherever they were supposed to be going. "Just a second, honey," she said sweetly to him before turning a baffled gaze to her. "You went to see the genie?"

"Yeah."

"Why?"

Gypsy perked a brow. "Why not? You know how much I love picking fights when the odds are against me."

"She did it for you," Cleos interjected.

"Excuse you." Gypsy glared back at Cleos, but he had no interest in her propriety.

Cori frowned at her. "The genie did that to you?"

"This?" Gypsy motioned to her injuries. "No, I did this."

"I walked in on her picking a fight with him." Cleos stepped out next to her. "I was finding the whole thing rather amusing until she tried to touch him."

"I did touch him," Gypsy declared, though there was no reward to be had from it.

"You touched the genie?" Cori's eyes grew large. "How could you... Why would you..."

"He wasn't accepting my offer."

"What offer?"

"Fair trade. My body for the kid's." Gypsy nodded to the little boy now hanging from her wrist like a swing. Cori stared blankly at her. "Seems only fair since I'm to blame for all of this. When I finally got a finger on him—"

"How are you still sane?" Cori asked, flabbergasted.

"I wasn't really sane to begin with, so I guess it didn't take."

"You should get yourself checked out," Cori suggested.

Gypsy made a clicking sound with her tongue and pointed to the infirmary entrance. "On my way."

"Right," Cori said absentmindedly. "Good." She walked away.

"Corinthia, we need to talk," Cleos called after her.

She turned back and looked at Cleos with tired eyes. "I'm spending some time with my son. We are going to go see the monkey." Cori smiled down at her son, who jumped up and down at the sound of the word alone. "Whatever you need to say can wait." Cori walked off, leaving Cleos to stare after her. The forlorn expression baffled Gypsy. Cleos was a fairly temperamental man, but she had never seen him looking so wistful.

"What's your deal with her?" Gypsy asked the question she had been waiting a long time to ask.

Cleos didn't look at her when he spoke; he just kept his eyes on the distance growing between him and Cori. "Some time ago, I made a mistake. A mistake that someday

Cori may have to suffer for. The longer I wait to tell her, the less chance I have of saving her." Cleos finally looked at her. "But the sooner I tell her, the sooner I will have to fight a battle I am not entirely sure I can win."

Gypsy shifted to look at him straight on. "You do realize that nothing you just said made any sense to me?"

"Yes."

"Whatever?" She strutted toward the infirmary, feeling all sorts of herself again. "I'm getting stitches; you wanna watch?"

"I'll be right behind you," he said.

When Gypsy got to the door of the infirmary, she looked back and saw that Cleos was leaning against the wall holding his forehead. She wasn't sure what was putting him in such a bad mood. What could be worse than a genie taking the form of a human? Surely nothing could be more urgent than the power of the sun and the moon being unleashed on the world.

16

Nurses and doctors rushed back and forth in the hallway ahead of Gypsy. She bypassed the nurse's station and followed the droning beep and piercing alarm that had everyone in a rush. As she rounded the corner onto another branch of the corridor, she could see the problem.

The doctor was shouting out for injections as he primed his electrical paddles. "Clear!" he shouted when the defibrillator signaled it was ready. Power shot through the chest of the elderly woman in the hospital bed. Everyone paused and stared at the monitor for signs of life.

Nothing.

"Clear!" the doctor demanded again.

Nothing.

The ringing sound of an unchanging heart monitor was all too familiar to Gypsy. She had tried for years to accept the role of a healer as a way of helping people, but there was no control in that field. Just as these men and women were powerless to save this old woman, she was powerless to save her patients.

Being powerless was unacceptable to her.

"I'm calling it." The doctor retreated from the woman. He rubbed his face and moved to the red phone on the wall. He picked it up and dialed a single number on the old-fashioned rotary dial. "Yeah," he responded as if the caller had already expected his call. "She's gone. Annette is dead."

Annette? Gypsy looked at the old woman again. Could that really be her? She looked nothing like she had before. Her previously blonde hair was pure white. Years had creased her face seemingly overnight.

"This really is a shit week," Gypsy mumbled and turned away from the door. She noticed Levi—Annette's Boy Wonder—standing in the hall staring down at the floor. She hadn't noticed him on the way in, which was odd since she must have passed right by him. "Hey, kid," she said, drawing his eyes up to her. "Tough break."

His eyes narrowed, and he shook his head. "How do you do it? How do you feel nothing?"

Gypsy smiled proudly, though she knew it was not the time to let her pride show. "Trust me, there's nothing inspirational about my story." Gypsy moved closer to him. He averted his gaze, concentrating back on his shoes. "You're a bit of a magical resource, aren't you?"

"Annette has taught me a lot."

"So, how do you propose we help Cori with her little genie problem?"

"They've already consulted me."

"And?"

"And I told them to give the child to him."

Gypsy laughed. "You can't be serious."

"A genie isn't a witch or sorcerer; it's an aberration of nature. It isn't a true being. You can't fight it. You can't negotiate with it."

"I understand that much already, but magic can be fought with magic, can't it?"

"A genie isn't magic, it's power. Power harnessed by the strength of dark magic." Gypsy rubbed her wrists where the memory of leather straps being tightened around them was still fresh. "Power that has been stripped of its purpose and design." She flinched, still feeling the pain of knives cutting her skin... *his* skin. "Injected with new rules." Gypsy tensed, resisting the overwhelming urge to scream right along with the man in her memories. "Are you okay?" Levi asked, his face scrunched more with disgust than concern.

"A vessel?"

"What?"

"The genie is a vessel, and the vessel is a man."

"No, there is no longer anything human left in him."

"But once upon a time," Gypsy snapped. "A long, long—long fucking time ago, there was a human vessel that they bound this power to."

"Yeah, I suppose they would have—"

"A child."

"Ah, I don't know who—"

"A little boy, not much older than ten."

"I have no idea."

"He was sacrificed so that his people could have better lives."

"Where are you getting this information?"

"Never mind that." Gypsy grabbed Levi's shoulder and ushered him down the hallway with her. "How do we veto the dark magic and send the power back up to the moon and the stars?"

"We don't."

"Come on, Levi, there has to be some uber spell that can be performed to unravel him. Some magic potion he can choke on."

"This isn't a Wiccan group playing with Ouji boards. This is life or death."

"Exactly, now can you conjure a demon, raise Screamin' Jay Hawkins from the dead, or do something useful to break this spell?"

Levi pushed away from her and shook his head. "This isn't a spell," Levi spoke scornfully. "It's a curse. A very powerful one. No one would have enough power to strip away bindings that have been in effect for thousands of years?"

"What about your girl?" Gypsy crossed her arms and leaned against the nearest wall. "Just theoretically speaking, would a sorceress have enough mojo to break the genie's chains?"

"You're still not getting this," Levi sighed in frustration. "It would take the strength of a dozen sorcerers to cut his ties to the earth. And I'm pretty sure the last time the earth saw anything akin to that was when the genie was made."

Gypsy blinked away the overlapping vision of a group of men and women circled around her. She could hear them whispering in her ears, but she couldn't understand the language at all. She tried to shake the voices away, but they were persistent. So much so that she batted at them like irritating flies.

Levi frowned at her. "I know you want to help—everyone does—but this isn't something to be fought. It's to be accepted."

"I should accept the complete and utter destruction of the Earth?"

Levi's face blanked and for a moment Gypsy thought she was looking into the cold stony face of her own reflection. He stepped forward, making her tense, although he was not nearly her physical equal. "Danato and the others have to assume the worst. That is their job. And most of the time, they would be right. But ask yourself why the universe would destroy its own creation. Why would the power of the universe—the very origin of life itself—seek to squelch life?"

"For the same reason that the earth spews lava and turns rainwater into floods. Nature is chaos. The world seeks to balance itself by whatever means necessary. Killing humans is a result of that chaos."

Levi shook his head. "Only when they get in the way." As he backed away, his fury dimmed, and he looked like himself again. Gypsy watched him walk back down the hall and into Annette's room. She stared after him for several seconds, trying to decide what it was she didn't like about this kid.

17

ORI HEARD A KNOCK on the front door so quiet that she waited for the second knock to confirm someone was at the door. She moved away from the cold breakfast that was serving as her lunch—or at least it would have if she had taken more than a few bites of it. She had been up all night with Ethan, Danato, and Belus trying to find a solution to her son's predicament. They had read through every text on the genie and considered every physical and magical source of protection—including the Medusa statue. They had even considered putting the poor child into a temporary coma, hoping the genie couldn't access him.

However, as the night grew long, the mood had shifted. Their efforts to avoid voicing the worst-case scenario widened the already expanding divide between Ethan and Danato. Though everyone was trying to remain hopeful for a positive outcome, the ticking clock was counting down to a death sentence, and they all knew it.

Although the arrival of their guests had irritated her, she was almost glad for it now. It gave them all permission to disband. She hadn't seen Danato since the meeting, and she honestly didn't expect to see him until he came for her son. Danato loved her son like his own grandchild, but if time ran out, he would come. And if he put the boy to death, she was certain that it would be his last official act as warden—one way or another.

Ethan was off trying to figure out how to use his mage power so he could stop all of this. She had wanted him by her side at first, but now as her hope dimmed, she knew looking into his still-optimistic eyes would break both of them, and she didn't want to spend her last hours with her son weeping.

Belus was keeping to himself as well. She suspected he was preparing for the possibility of unburdening Danato once again from his duty. Though if history was any indicator, it didn't matter who pulled the trigger—everyone was going to get hurt. She wasn't sure how this day would end, but she was certain her relationship with her family would never be the same when it did. And neither would her heart.

Cori opened the front door. Leona looked back at her, just as surprised to see her on the other side. The house cooled a few degrees, and Cori's face settled into an unwelcoming frown. "What are you doing here?"

Leona put on a tight smile before answering. "I came to see Danato."

"He's not here." Cori started to close the door, but Leona pressed her hand to it, stopping it from closing.

"Actually, the reason for my visit is about you."

"Me?"

"May I come in and speak with you?" Cori's eyes narrowed on her. She didn't have time for an argument. "I only wish to converse with you civilly. No tricks." She held up her hands in surrender.

Cori gave in and moved back to the island, leaving the door open for Leona to come in. The fem-wolf stepped through the door carefully, as if the floor might be unsteady. She gently closed the door behind her and took a moment to look around the home—as one does when one first arrives in a strange place. Her judgmental trepidation seemed to melt as she took in the clean, rustic features of the house. It was by no means a mansion, but it was a fine home. A small smile perched on her lips, as if she were thinking about something—maybe a memory.

"What do you want?" Cori asked before shoveling bacon and eggs into her mouth. She suddenly felt starved. She didn't bother sitting down at the island or table; she just hovered over the counter in the kitchen, ignoring all eating etiquette.

Leona rubbed her hands together and moved a little closer to speak. She opened her mouth, but the words didn't come out. She turned away, then back, and tried again. Her mouth hung open, her tongue darting to her teeth as if she were contemplating a complex math problem.

"Leona, I'm not psychic."

She nodded and cleared her throat. "I know what you must think of me." She paused, as if allowing Cori the opportunity to insert some adjectives. "I think that when a woman tries to surpass expectations, she can often come off as..."

"A bitch?" Cori suggested.

Leona's face hardened, but only for a moment, then she looked disappointed. "Yes, I think that would be the description. The thing is, now that I am exactly the woman I wanted to be, I sometimes wish that I were another kind of woman."

"Good to know." Cori finished her food and rinsed her plate off. "Is there a point to this?"

"My point is, you and I will be seeing more of each other now, and I don't want there to be any ill will for my past indiscretions."

"Indiscretions?" Cori scoffed. "Other than forcing my ex to cheat on me and trying to rape my husband? Not to mention just being a vindictive bitch to me."

"What I am trying to say is I don't want to be that person anymore?"

"Just because you want to change, doesn't mean I have to."

"I'm not saying you need to change. I'm saying, I need to change."

"And you want what in return? For me to forget about how you've behaved in the past?"

"Not forget, but at least not focus on it so much."

Cori approached Leona and crossed her arms. "I don't know what Cleos has told you—"

"Nothing," Leona snapped. "He doesn't share your memories with me."

Cori wondered why he didn't give Leona her memories, but meanwhile Gypsy seemed to have her autobiography.

"I didn't come here to pick a fight. I came here to tell Danato that I will try my best to get along with you, for the sake of our mutual interests. I can see now that you are going to make that very difficult for me."

"*I* make that difficult?"

"So," Leona spoke louder over the top of her. "I will just have to try harder because I know that what we are trying to accomplish here is more important than my pride."

Cori stared at her, head shaking slightly even though she wasn't responding to anything. "I don't trust you, Leona."

Leona nodded, dismal disappointment taking over her features. "I know."

Before Cori could respond, the door to the house flung open and Gypsy came rushing inside. She did a double take on Leona before she landed her determined eyes on Cori. "You need to get out of here."

"What?" Cori barely had time to get the question out before the woman was running toward the staircase.

"Gypsy, get out." Cori followed her when she realized she had no intention of stopping. "What are you doing?"

"Which one is yours?" Gypsy jogged up the staircase and looked around at the closed doors.

"Why are you here?" Cori should have been screaming at her, but she was past the point of feeling anger. She was past the point of feeling anything.

Gypsy opened one of the spare bedrooms before she found Cori and Ethan's apartment. She invited herself inside and headed straight for the closet. Cori watched her dig through the shelves until she found a duffle bag. She looked over the endless line of black t-shirts before she reached the multicolored spectrum that belonged to her. She grabbed a fistful of cloth and yanked them off the hangers. A couple of pairs of jeans disappeared into the bag, along with socks, underwear, and a bra from her lingerie drawer.

"Grace, what on earth are you doing?" Leona asked when she arrived on the scene.

Gypsy looked up at them both with determination. "Do you have a diaper bag or something?" She pushed past Cori and headed into the bathroom. Cori considered yelling about the invasion of her privacy. The woman's behavior shocked her, but she was also curious.

Cori peeked in the bathroom and watched Gypsy scavenge the drawers for necessities: deodorant, toothpaste—she even grabbed a handful of makeup, though Cori assumed she had no idea what she was grabbing. Gypsy's idea of makeup was lip gloss and mascara. "What are you doing?" Cori tried asking one more time.

Gypsy looked up at her when the bag was full. "Grab the kid and meet me on the roof."

"Why?" Cori put her arm across the doorway before Gypsy could leave the bathroom.

Gypsy stopped in front of her, lording her dark eyes over her. "You and the boy need to get out of here. It's going to be a long ride, so pee if you need to."

"Don't be ridiculous, Grace. You can't outrun a genie."

"I'm not worried about the Genie. I'm worried about Danato." Gypsy stared Cori down hard. "He will kill the child, Cori. I know you think he won't, but he will. Danato will do his duty."

Cori sputtered out a small laugh, but it soon died away. "You think I don't know that? You think that I'm deluding myself into thinking that he will spare my baby. I know what he has to do. I've known since the moment I told him."

"Then don't give him the option. You still have a few hours left until this god-forsaken place stops chasing the sun. Maybe when you and I are in the wind, he'll work a little harder on a solution that doesn't involve infanticide."

Cori's lip perked up into a crooked smile. "Okay." She put down her arm, and Gypsy bolted from the room.

Cori turned to fetch her son, but Leona pressed her hand on her chest. "You know you can't do this. There is too much at stake."

"I know," Cori said but proceeded to flop her sleeping little boy over her shoulder. She put a heavy blanket over him to shield him from the elements and carried him downstairs.

Leona followed behind her, at first quietly, but when they left the house, she found her voice again. "I can't imagine what you are going through. A decision without a choice is unbearable, but I think you know the difference between a solution and an evasion."

"Why aren't you stopping me if you don't agree with me?" Cori asked.

Leona took a deep breath and released it. "It is not my place to decide the fate of another woman's child."

"But it is Danato's?" Cori asked more philosophically than accusatory.

Leona frowned and looked forward. She didn't say another word.

By the time Cori and Leona reached the roof, Gypsy was screaming at her helicopter and banging on the dials. Cori grimaced, already guessing the problem. She set down her son and pulled the blanket around him before approaching the chopper and the cussing woman now hanging out of the engine. "It won't start, will it?" Cori inquired.

Gypsy looked back at her; eyes narrowed at Cori's complete lack of surprise. It was an interesting role reversal; she thought. Gypsy was going berserk while Cori maintained her composure. It wouldn't last, but it was nice to be the calm one for once.

"Ethan and I tried to escape earlier this morning. Not long before you arrived. The gates had been locked on Danato's orders. He was one step ahead of us. I'm willing to hazard a guess that he has removed something vital from your chopper... just in case."

"Danato did this?" Gypsy slipped out of the engine and looked around for something that she wasn't likely to find on that roof. "He's trapped you here."

Cori's mouth tipped up slightly, and she shook her head. "You think you know how far he will go... You have no idea, Gypsy."

"We'll find another way."

"Why is this so important to you?"

"Why isn't it important to you?"

"It is, but I can't fight a genie."

Gypsy shook her head. "What's wrong with you?" Gypsy snarled and grabbed her shoulders. "This isn't you!" She shook her.

"Grace, leave her alone," Leona scolded.

"Where is Cori? Where is the woman that I had to dismember before she would quit? Where is she!"

"She's dying inside!" Cori lost control of her composure, but she didn't fall to pieces like she wanted to.

"I'm on the verge of collapse and I need to find a solution, but the minute I start looking at those books I just think about what I'm losing. So, you tell me what I should do, Gypsy. Hold on to hope as it slips through my fingers or hold on to my son for as long as I can." Cori nodded back to her son, who was oblivious to the countdown on his life.

"This can't end this way!" Gypsy shook her harder. Leona moved in closer and rested her hand on Gypsy's—almost protectively.

"It can, and it will, unless you have a miracle in your back pocket."

Gypsy frowned and shook her head. "I want to help, Cori. Tell me what to do."

"There's nothing to do."

"Yes, there is! There always is!"

"We have done nothing but try to think of options."

"There is something you haven't thought of because it's too dangerous or against Danato's rules or just downright insane. What is it?"

Cori tried to think, but her mind was useless. Every thought was of her boy and the man or men that were about to kill him to save him from possession. Nothing in the prison was strong enough to defend against a genie. Nothing could break a contract with a god.

"What is it, Cori?" Gypsy's insistence was irritating her. She just wanted to be left alone with her son. "Search the dark recesses of your mind. What is it that you absolutely cannot do? If you find it and I will do it for you. What do you need?"

"Do you know what I need? I need more time with my son. Can you do that, Gypsy?"

"Fine! Then let's summon Kronos so I can kick his ass and I will get you more time."

"Then you do that, Gypsy," Cori said mockingly. "Wave your magic wand and give me more TIME!"

Cori could feel a shiver of cold crawling out of Gypsy's fingers and up her arm, but she couldn't move. By the time the flicker of light that followed it hit her, she was already feeling sick to her stomach. A twist in her vision, followed by a sharp drop did the trick, and she heaved.

After several lurches and two failed attempts to bring up food, Cori looked around trying to understand what had just happened to her. She quickly allayed suspicions of an attack when she realized that Gypsy was beside her, just as sick as she was. She looked at Leona on her other side. She was lying on her back holding her stomach. By the looks of the puddle beside her, she had succeeded in bringing up her last meal.

"Graaaace!" Leona yowled and looked past Cori to Gypsy. "What did you dooooo?"

Gypsy was hunched over, spitting out the residue in her mouth. When she looked back at Leona, she grimaced. "What are you talking about?"

"I feel like I just took a turn on the dance floor at jet speed," Leona complained.

"And how is that my fault?" Gypsy asked.

"I don't know, but you are usually to blame for my misery."

Cori shook her head. "It happened to all three of us. Something..."

"What?" Gypsy asked.

"I don't know. It felt like magic. Like that tingling sensation I would get in my fingers when my rings would start working."

"You did this?" Leona accused her.

"No, my rings aren't working anymore." Cori glanced at her hands, but she already knew where the magic had emanated from. "It came from Gypsy."

Gypsy stared blankly back at her. "Me?"

"Yes, I told you to give me more time, and then your hands—"

"See! It's always you."

Gypsy glared at Leona. "Are you suggesting that I cast a spell to make us all sick?"

"No, but maybe you..." Cori turned around in search of something to support her theory. There wasn't much to see around the prison. The breeze was gone, and the few clouds left in the sky weren't moving. She looked at the dim blue light in the sky that was only going to get darker.

Cori moved to her son and pulled back the blanket. She found him curled in a ball, still asleep. However, the longer she watched him, the stranger he looked. He was too still.

Cori clucked at him and rubbed his arm to stir him, but he didn't move. Leona and Gypsy joined her inspection. "Is he..." Leona asked.

"No," Gypsy said, checking for a pulse. "But..."

"What?"

"The pulse is... I felt it, but then it was gone," Gypsy said.

"Look there." Leona pointed to a rash forming on the child's arm where Cori had recently touched the child. "What is that? Is this the genie?"

"My time isn't up yet," Cori whispered.

"There," Gypsy said. "I felt it again. It's so slow. Let's get him down to the infirmary."

Cori didn't argue with that plan. She hoisted the boy into her arms and followed Gypsy and Leona to the stairwell. She had hoped the elevator would arrive promptly at the upper floor to take them downstairs, but they ended up taking the stairs instead.

"Something feels wrong." Leona was the first to say it as they descended the stairs, but Cori was thinking it as well, and judging by the way Gypsy kept looking around, she was likely feeling it too. "I can't quite—wait. Someone is following us."

Gypsy looked up, reaching for her gun, but since Ethan had relieved her of it earlier, she could only grope her holster. They all paused, listening for more footsteps, but they didn't continue. "Was someone on the upper floor?"

"It could be anyone," Cori said. "Let's keep moving." She continued on but ignored the drum-like clunk of footsteps that followed just behind them down the stairwell. Whoever was following them was staying out of view for some reason. She didn't care about the stalkers. She just needed to check on her son.

When they finally arrived at the infirmary level, Cori felt a wave of humidity much as she usually did. The vague smell of manure was never a welcome smell, but sadly she would forever associate the contrary odor with tongue depressors and morphine. A sound she couldn't quite place replaced the usually loud chirping of birds, but she didn't stop to inquire about the change in tune.

She ran to the infirmary and pushed the door open. The pressure against her hand released as she broke through the glass. It turned to pebbles before her eyes and slowly fell to the ground like floating snow.

"What just happened?" Cori looked back at the two women coming up behind her. They looked at the shattered glass and then exchanged a worried glance.

"Have you been working out, dear?" Leona asked.

"Not that much." Cori nodded at the broken door.

"Forget the door." Gypsy stepped through the opening and marched toward the nurse's hub, where Ethan, Efrat, and Levi were standing around chatting. "Boys, have you been experiencing anything weird?" she asked, but none of them responded.

Cori followed her in with Leona carefully maneuvering her heels through the glass behind her. "Ethan, there is something wrong with our son." Ethan didn't even turn away from his conversation with Efrat. "Ethan."

"Cori." Gypsy looked back at her. "I think whatever is going on with that kid is happening to them. Look." Gypsy waved her hand in front of Ethan's face. She did the same to Efrat before scooting past Levi to get back to her. "I think I know what this is."

"What?" Cori asked.

"I think we've somehow stopped time."

"How?"

"I don't know." Gypsy propped her hands up on her hips. "Well..." Her face scrunched up tight as if she smelled something rotten. "I might have an idea."

"What?" Cori narrowed her eyes at Gypsy. "What did you do this time?"

"Why does everyone assume I did something?"

"Because, Grace, you are a nuisance." Leona grabbed Cori's shoulder to balance her while she flicked the glass off the bottom of her shoe. With some effort, Cori stayed upright against the pressure the fem-wolf was putting on her.

"I'm not immune to bad luck, you know? And this place is full of bad juju."

"Just tell us what you think happened," Cori said impatiently.

"I think I caught something from that sorceress?" Gypsy asked.

"Eww!" Leona wrinkled her nose. "What do lesbian lovers have to do with this?"

Gypsy's face blanked, legitimately shocked by Leona's inference of STDs.

"She's talking about an actual sorceress," Cori clarified.

"A real sorceress? Who the fuck made one of those?"

"Long story," Cori said. "I'm surprised Cleos didn't tell you."

"Aww, poor Cori. I know it's difficult for you to share the men in your life, but you can't have them all to yourself."

"You can have him," she mumbled.

"Don't worry, Cleos only shares information pertinent to his mission," Gypsy said. "He likes to keep us... on our toes."

"What did you mean you caught something from Addy?" Cori asked.

"I'm not sure. I got some of her blood on me, and since then I've had some issues."

"This better not be contagious," Leona said unimpressed.

"Not those kinds of issues, you twit," Gypsy snapped. "Her blood was glowing—imbued or something. I knew the minute it got into my system, something wasn't right. And since then..."

"What is it?" Cori frowned.

Gypsy shifted uncomfortably. "I'd rather not say."

"Why?" Cori wondered what could possibly put the hollow-hearted woman so on edge.

"Yes, why?" Leona moved a little closer and sniffed her. Gypsy swatted at her but didn't budge. Leona gasped and took another whiff. "Oh, good Lord, is that shame I smell?"

"I am not ashamed of something I can't control."

"Oh, but that's just it." Leona circled her, grinning from ear to ear. "Grace Gypsum, the powerhouse of stone, is ashamed of her lack of control. Let's see, what could this sorceress give you to make you..." Leona stopped and stared at Gypsy. The woman glared at her, jaw clenched, not wanting to reveal her secrets. "No. It can't be." Leona took a step back to look over the rest of her. "Grace," she said quietly. "Have you contracted... feelings?"

Gypsy gnashed her teeth before answering. "Yes."

Leona raised her head and let out a breathy laugh.

"They aren't my feelings. What the hell!" Gypsy turned and pushed Leona out of her way as best she could. Given the high heels, Leona was a bit like a hippo on roller skates at the moment. She grabbed the counter of the nurse's station to stay upright. Instead of retaliating against Gypsy, she continued to stare in the direction of the men.

"That's not right," Leona said more to herself than to either of them.

"What is it?" Cori didn't immediately notice the problem. Not until she felt the eyes on her. Then she couldn't unsee it. Ethan and Efrat were now staring in their direction instead of at each other. Their stillness gave the impression of mannequins, which made their change in position seem almost eerie. "Ethan?" she asked again, hoping that he could hear her.

"Why are they moving, Grace?" Leona said. "I thought you said we stopped time."

"Like I have a rule book on this stuff. Maybe they are just moving really slowly. What are they looking at?" Cori and Gypsy spread apart and looked at the entrance. No one was coming in. No one was going out. What had drawn their attention?

"I don't know," Cori said.

Leona looked back, and her shoulders dropped. "Ugh, you idiots, they are looking at the door." Leona pointed with a lazy finger. "If they are moving slowly, then they are just now reacting to the noise of the door breaking."

"If they can hear the glass break, why not us?" Cori asked.

"They probably can, but we sound like a buzzing fly because we are talking so fast."

"The footsteps in the stairwell," Gypsy said. "The sound was moving slower for us. Those were our footsteps."

"That's why his pulse feels so slow," Cori said with some relief. "He's fine, but to us, it feels elongated."

Gypsy looked at Cori even more befuddled than when they started their explanation of the events. "Does that even make sense? Has all time slowed or just here at the prison?"

"What difference does it make?" Leona asked.

Gypsy looked at Cori with notable empathy. "Because if it's only the prison, then the clock is still counting. If it's the clock, then we have more time to help Cori."

"Oh," Leona looked at Cori guiltily and then gave her a small smile.

"Don't be nice, Leona."

"What? Why?"

"Because you being nice to me is like being served a death sentence. If you're in good cheer, then I must be on my deathbed."

"Oh, fine!" Leona threw up her hands. "You want me to be honest? I want to get out of this time lock as soon as possible because I don't want to be stuck with the two of you any longer than necessary."

"I think it's safe to say that we have never had more in common," Cori retorted.

"Ladies, as much as I hate being the mediator, I do think it is in our best interest to call a truce while we are dealing with this predicament."

"Does that mean you won't try to chop anyone's body parts off?" Leona crossed her arms.

Gypsy's mouth tipped up into a smirk. "Only if the aforementioned parts don't piss me off. So maybe you should shut your lips."

"Go ahead." Leona puckered her lips. Gypsy cracked her neck but didn't take the bait. "What's wrong, Grace? Is the bit getting caught in your teeth?"

"I wish you knew how many times that bit has saved your life?"

"What are you talking about?" Cori asked.

"Oh, hasn't Cleos told you yet?" Leona asked Cori conspiratorially.

"Leona, shut up," Gypsy seethed and even made a move to grab Leona, but she jumped out of her reach, giggling on the way.

"If you want to get any shots in, Cori, now is the time."

Gypsy followed Leona, breathing heavy breaths as she stalked her. "Shut up, you hairy mutt!"

"What are you talking about?" Cori followed their slow chase into the waiting area.

"Cleos knows how volatile Grace can be, so he muzzled her—" Leona ducked a punch from Gypsy. Following the attack, Gypsy grabbed her forehead and groaned in pain. "—and put her on a leash." Leona laughed manically.

"What does that mean?"

Leona's amusement settled, and she wiped tears from her eyes. She moved to Cori and looked at Gypsy condescendingly. "Grace cannot hurt either one of us—unless it's necessary to save our lives—thus, unfortunately, your hand."

"Cleos put a mandate in her mind?"

"Yes, and defying it is very uncomfortable." Gypsy glared at both of them, panting and ready to attack, but according to Leona, she couldn't. "See there, you thought that Cleos didn't care about you, but he still does." Leona reached across and took her son off her hands. "Go on, Cori. Take your shot while you still can."

"But earlier we were fighting just fine."

"Oh, she can defend herself if you attack her, but she is limited to the necessity of defense. If she tries to do more than subdue you, she will be in a great amount of pain."

Cori knew that Leona's goading was purely self-serving and that fighting Gypsy at this moment was not likely to solve anything. However, without Cleos or Danato to interject, this was likely the only chance she would have to satisfy her concerns about this woman's unwelcome presence in her life.

As if sensing her rising hackles, Gypsy's glare flattened, and she leveled her dead eyes on Cori. At that moment, she knew in her heart of hearts that she was empty. Her nemesis was nothing more than a serial killer perpetually on the verge of a murder spree.

Cori shifted her stance and balled her fists. Years of pain came out of nowhere, feeding her rage and eliminating her denial. It didn't even matter that most of her anguish started before Gypsy was ever in her life. She wanted a scapegoat in the form of a punching bag, and her face would do nicely. She moved forward, and Gypsy began the dance, drawing herself down and raising her own fists to prepare for a fight.

They circled each other, putting her right in Leona's path. The fem-wolf smiled and lifted her leg. She kicked forward, burying her high heel in the small of Gypsy's back. She winced and cried out as she stumbled toward Cori. She immediately turned back, ready to get revenge on Leona, but the fem-wolf clucked her tongue and shook her finger. "No, no, no, I have the child."

While Gypsy was growling over Leona's home-base status, Cori reached down and yanked the knife out of Gypsy's calf holster. Cori barely had time to get it out before a fist landed on her temple. She fell back, landing on a set of chairs that scattered in her wake.

Gypsy held her forehead, incapacitated by her punishment for an unnecessary level of violence. It wasn't a fair fight, by any means, but Cori no longer cared about the right or wrong of it. She jumped back up and slashed the knife left and right, ready to cut the woman open and pull out her blackened heart. Gypsy narrowly avoided each slash.

Leona laughed. "Better run, Grace, I think she wants your hand."

Gypsy glanced at Leona. "Shut up!"

Cori took advantage of the distraction and kicked Gypsy in the stomach. She hit the wall and dented the drywall before rebounding to attack. Cori ducked and flipped the woman over her shoulder. She landed hard on the floor and coughed. Cori jumped on top of her and thrust the knife down at her. Gypsy barely got her hands beneath Cori's wrists before the tip hit her breast.

"Cori," Leona was no longer amused by the fight. She had not intended for her to take out years of pain on Gypsy.

Gypsy panted beneath her, struggling to get the upper hand on her. Despite the woman's more muscular arms, Cori had the upper hand, and she knew how to use her weight to her advantage. They locked eyes as Gypsy's face shifted into an emotion easily confused for fear. Though Cori suspected Gypsy was capable of fear, this was something best described as certainty. The realization that death was about to come and there was nothing she could do about it.

Cori shifted higher, putting all of her weight over the knife. She would have no trouble pressing the blade into her heart. Nor would she have any regrets about removing Gypsy Grace from this earth. There was nothing that could stop her except a single spoken word.

"Stop."

18

IT WASN'T YELLED OR spoken in a demanding voice. It was just a feather floating down between them, making the world seem normal again. The anger inside Cori shrank away—not disappearing, but just going dormant for now. At that moment, Cori was staring down at a woman instead of an enemy.

The pain lingered a bit longer, but she couldn't remember why she wanted to blame Gypsy for it. It certainly wasn't her fault that her father virtually abandoned her. Gypsy didn't grow the cancer inside of her mother. She didn't make the world nefarious and conniving. She was just another employee caught up in the world of the supernatural. She may have been emotionally unstable, but Gypsy wasn't the one about to commit murder.

Gypsy pushed her wrists away, leaving behind a small rent in her black t-shirt, revealing a little blood. When she was clear of the danger, she flipped Cori off with ease and reached for her gun. She clawed at her empty holster before growling and leaping to her feet. She grabbed Levi by his neck and shoved him back against the wall. "Where the hell did you come from?"

Levi choked in her tight grip and pointed to where he had previously been standing near Ethan and Efrat.

"How are you able to move with us?"

Levi coughed and started turning red.

"You have to let him breathe if you want him to answer, Grace." Leona moved to the pair and removed Gypsy's hand with very little effort. She gave up her attack and began pacing the waiting area. "There you are, young man. Just take a few breaths." Leona patted Levi's back while he coughed through his next inhalations. She turned to Cori and frowned. "I was only kidding, Cori," she scolded before helping her to her feet. "I didn't think you would try to kill her."

"I just got..." Cori trailed off, not wanting to answer for her actions. She didn't want to admit that the last few days had left her feeling unhinged and barely able to focus on anything beyond her anguish.

"Now what were you saying—er..." Leona leaned into Cori and whispered. "What's his name?"

"This is Levi. He was assisting Annette... until recently."

"Oh? She was the witch, right?"

"Yes."

"That is good," Leona declared. "Now we have someone to help us."

Levi rose back up to full height before speaking. "I'm sorry. I didn't mean to scare you."

Gypsy glared at him. "You didn't scare me. You just surprised me. Did Ethan give you lessons on that sneaky shit or what?"

"It's not my fault. People just forget that I'm here sometimes. I try not to take offense."

"Levi, how are you not affected by the slowing of time?" Cori asked.

"I'm immune to magic." Levi rubbed his neck. "I wasn't sure what had happened, so when you came in, I just acted like I was frozen. I wasn't trying to be sneaky." Levi glanced at Gypsy. "I was just observing the situation."

Gypsy continued to pace back and forth, seemingly trying to walk off her frustration. "You mean spy on our conversation for a while."

"Give it a rest, Grace," Leona scolded her.

"Levi, do you have any thoughts on what Gypsy said earlier?" Cori asked. "Why are we stuck outside of time?"

"If she had been exposed to dark magic, she could have invoked a spell."

"A spell?" Gypsy waved her hands and came back into the group. "I didn't do a spell. I didn't say a single abracadabra. I just said that I wanted to give Cori more time."

"And you meant it, didn't you?" Levi asked.

Gypsy gave Cori a fleeting look as if she were embarrassed to admit the sincerity of her offer. "Yeah, so?"

"Those that conjure power like Annette must perform complex rituals with magically infused objects or ingredients—like dragon's blood. However, those with inner magic. Those that house the power within them can alter the world around them with an ardent request or strong desire."

"So, Grace really did cast a spell?" Leona asked.

"Yes, she did."

"Oh, son of a bitch!" Gypsy snapped before walking out of the infirmary.

19

"How do we reverse it?" Cori asked Levi as they all headed down to the main floor. At Levi's suggestion, they opted to leave the boy in the infirmary since the child was more likely to get hurt by them than on his own. Gypsy wasn't a fan of having the child out of her sight since he currently had a demi-god and an ogre after him, but so long as time was in slow mode, there was time to get back before the clock ran out. Assuming time was actually moving slower, which Gypsy found highly unlikely.

She knew the world was full of strange magical phenomena, but even so. If she followed the rules of dark magic, then she would have the most influence over other beings—animals, entities, or possibly even man-made mechanisms. To alter the flow of time should have been beyond her ability—unless it wasn't dark magic that the sorceress dumped in her. Could it be? Was Gypsy the new Mother Earth?

"That's up to her." Levi motioned back to her. "She just has to want to put time back as it was and say so."

Everyone stopped in the stairwell and looked at Gypsy. She shrugged and raised her hands to the heavens theatrically. "Great Kronos, bring back the tick of the clock."

When nothing sensational happened, Levi shook his head. "You have to mean it."

"Don't you want the time back?" Cori asked, with an accusation already lying in wait.

"Sure, just not until we have a plan for the genie."

Cori's argument died before it could reach her lips. "Why are you so concerned about that? You can't possibly care about anyone—let alone a child you barely know."

Gypsy stared at Cori trying to decide if there was any point in explaining her moratorium on hurting children. Never mind that it was the only thing keeping her from slipping off the dark edge of psychosis and into the cold waters of murder for hire. Or worse—murder for free. No one understood the struggle that she faced to keep her pleasures in check. Well, perhaps there was one who understood. And he described it best: "...this *is* me controlling my damn self."

Gypsy rolled her shoulders. "I guess it's just part of Cleos's protection clause. Can't let you girls get hurt, remember? And I'm pretty sure losing that boy will hurt you."

"Never mind what her motivations are," Leona said to Cori. "As much as I hate to admit it. If Grace is on your side, then you just count yourself lucky and move on."

"Aww, that was almost sweet, Leo," Gypsy smirked at the fem-wolf.

"Don't call me that, and it doesn't mean I like you. It just means you are useful... at times. This not being one of them." Leona motioned to the proverbial predicament she had gotten them into before stomping down the stairs.

Gypsy smiled after her until she saw the look of confusion on Cori's face. The woman legitimately didn't like her, didn't trust her, and obviously wanted her dead, but she was still obsessed with her. Trying to figure out what makes her tick—what makes her tock. Gypsy tromped down a few steps to her, letting her boots hit hard and heavy on every step. The effect was somewhat downplayed by the delayed sound of the impact and its echo, but nonetheless it was a little creepy. She stopped at the step just above Cori, towering over her. Cori didn't flinch or release her gaze. Gypsy liked that. She preferred Cori this way—stubborn and stupid. "You really do want me dead, don't you?"

"Yes," Cori answered honestly.

"Why? And don't give me any of that crap about the altered timeline, because you and I both know that I got fucked just as hard in that version of things as you did in this one."

Cori's eyes flickered over her for a moment. "Because I'm afraid that someday you're going to be my enemy again. I would rather save myself the trouble and just kill you now."

Gypsy nodded. She had to respect that answer, if for no other reason than it showed that Cori was a better judge of character than most people. She sat down on the steps, rather than continue to overshadow her. "You ever hear those stories about wild animals that befriend their prey?"

Cori didn't answer.

"You ever hear the stories about wild animals that were raised as pets, but then go crazy and maul their owners?"

Again, Cori didn't answer.

"Just think of me as somewhere in between those two scenarios." Gypsy stood and moved around her, positioning herself on the step next to her. She pressed into her space, breathing her air and making the tension between them seem more sexual than aggressive. "If you're so afraid of me becoming your enemy, then why do you keep trying to be mine?" Gypsy headed down the stairs, leaving Cori to consider how stupid it was to poke a bear.

20

ORI SLIPPED INTO THE office and found Danato at his desk and Belus sitting across from him. The big man was looking up at the clock while Belus was staring at the floor. It was only a matter of time before they tried to retrieve her son. They wouldn't wait until the last minute. There was too much at stake and too many barriers in their path.

Neither of them looked happy. She knew no one was comfortable with the decision being put before them. Who would be?

A question had been rolling around in her head since this all began.

Was it worth it?

She had left behind a world of normalcy and sought out this dangerous and strange world. She had effectively killed her mother to return to it, and now it would seem that she had killed her son as well. Just so she could have the life that she desired. She had chosen Ethan and Danato over her mother and son. It seems now that she would have been just as well off choosing the singular sacrifice instead of the three minor inconveniences. Or she could have stayed with her mother and raised her son with a man she didn't love. At least everyone would still be alive.

Cori stared at the clock a moment, listening to the tick-tock that didn't match the second hand. She felt her heart beat in rhythm with it. The sensation was strangely hypnotic. No longer irritating as she had once thought it. Just a slow, relaxing *tick, tick, tick*.

"Cori?" Levi asked from the door. She snapped out of her thoughts and looked at him. He glanced at the clock, then back at her. "What is it?"

"Nothing. I was just thinking that we have even less time than we think. He knows that there is a fight waiting for him."

Levi glanced out the door before stepping into the office. "There is something you could do. Something to stop this," he said rather conspiratorially.

"Like what?" Cori asked, hope pushing into her numb heart.

Levi nodded to Danato. "He's right here. He's barely moving. We have the advantage."

Cori smiled at Levi's enthusiasm for his intrigue. "What do you want me to do—hog-tie them? I doubt there is a binding strong enough to contain Danato for long."

"You could do something to slow him down." Cori stayed quiet, not wanting to assume that Levi was saying what she thought he was. "There are plenty of ways to incapacitate him without permanent harm."

Cori blinked at him, surprised that the young man, known to bring calmness to a room, was suggesting foul play to keep her son safe. "You know I love Danato, right?"

Levi nodded. "But your son—"

"Is safe for the time being."

"Cori," Levi whispered. "Whatever Gypsy did won't last long. We may not have this opportunity again. If you are planning to fight for your son's life, we need to find you an advantage over them."

Cori felt her stomach churn with unease. She couldn't imagine being forced to fight Danato or Belus. She wanted so much just to crawl into a hole and not come out until everything was better again. But if this week had taught her anything, it was that not every death sentence is escapable.

The problem, of course, was that Danato was a formidable enemy. There would be no running or hiding from him. And the only way to stop him from doing his duty was to do as Levi said and incapacitate him or kill him.

There had to be another way.

Cori looked down at her hands and the rings that could have solved this entire problem. She could just put Danato and Belus to sleep—the entire prison if necessary. Then, she and Ethan could run away with their son. Assuming, of course, he didn't turn into an all-powerful megalomaniac and kill them instead.

"Do you really think the genie would have good intentions?"

"I don't know about good, but he won't destroy the world. The entire point of becoming a human is for him to enjoy it."

"But what if Belus is right? What if the transformation to a human form makes him susceptible to human thoughts and emotions? How dangerous is a two-year-old with cosmic powers?"

Levi frowned and shook his head. "We can't know anything for certain, but..." He looked at Danato. "...looking at the world through the lens of this prison isn't always the best indicator of truth."

"What do you mean?"

"I mean that this place just scratches the surface of the supernatural world. Danato has been trained to turn his back on magic instead of understanding it. Annette was far more open-minded about these things."

Cori resisted the urge to point out that Annette's open-mindedness had also led to a volatile coven and the death of an innocent young girl. She understood what Levi was trying to say. While Annette may have been a little too free-spirited when it came to toying with magic, Danato was on the other end of the spectrum. He buried or destroyed anything that he considered too powerful. He would have burned the entire contents of the prop room, had it been possible to do so safely. He was probably secretly happy that her rings were no longer working.

"Belus thought that because Ethan created the spell for my rings, all I would have to do is add more magic to them. Do you think that would work? Can they be recharged?"

Levi pinched his lips as he considered this. "It depends if the rings are a cache or a repository. The spell could have simply programmed the power within. In that case, the rings are like the wand. After the power is gone, the object becomes inert. However, if the object itself is a totem, then it could theoretically just require some kind of magical inducement."

"Is there any way to give my rings a boost?"

"Possibly?" Levi frowned. "It's just not going to be easy. Come on." Levi motioned for her to follow him, and they headed back to the main foyer, where Gypsy was leaning against a wall and Leona was pacing the floor in front of the elevators.

"Aren't you cold?" the fem-wolf rubbed her arms.

"No, because I'm fully clothed," Gypsy answered.

"At least I do not look like a GI Joe," Leona snapped at her.

Gypsy shook her head unimpressed. "When are you going to figure out how to insult me? You're just embarrassing both of us at this point." Gypsy noted Cori's arrival and pushed off the wall. "What's the plan?"

"We are going to try to restore the power to Cori's rings," Levi announced.

Gypsy's face muddled with irritation. "Great, I'll be sure to keep my burn kit nearby."

"Can you do that?" Leona asked.

"We're going to try, but it's not going to be easy. We need to get some blood from the dragon."

"Why is that so hard?" Gypsy asked. "I was under the impression that you tapped her juices pretty regularly."

"Because the dragons have created a magical barrier around Addy's grave. It's likely that they won't be affected by the time shift. But it's also unlikely that they will simply stop praying just so you can soak your rings."

"Praying?" Gypsy perked a brow. "Dragons can pray?"

"It's a sort of coma state in which they combine mental energy in order to achieve a task."

"What are they trying to achieve?"

"I'm not sure exactly. I had hoped at one point that they might be trying to bring Addy back, but... that's a foolish hope."

"Bring her back?" Gypsy glanced at Cori, probably to see if she knew about this option, which she didn't. "Are you seriously talking about bringing people back from the dead now? If this place starts crawling with zombies, I am so out."

"Is that possible?" Cori looked at him expectantly. She wasn't thinking about Addy. She was actually thinking about Daniel. If the dragons could bring him back to life, maybe he could stop the genie. With Daniel, they would have real power.

Levi took a deep breath and shook his head. "No, not really. I mean, not in the way that you think. Resurrection spells are not easy with contrary magics. And besides, they are notoriously difficult to achieve on damaged bodies. It was a long shot for me to think Addy could be saved." Levi paused and looked at the floor. "Daniel would also be much too damaged to even consider it."

"What do you mean, contrary magics?" Gypsy asked.

"It's complicated," Levi said.

"I got a minute," Gypsy said, as she mockingly checked her imaginary wristwatch.

Levi looked at her, possibly searching for an objection, but Cori was actually curious about this as well. And since she was desperate for any shred of hope, any knowledge he could give might be helpful in the long run.

"Annette..." Levi paused after speaking her name as if just saying it made his emotions raw. "...would speak about the magical world as spheres. Some spheres are inside of each other like elemental power is to earth power. They are the same but separate. Cosmic power like the genie's is outside of the earth, but touches it. They are related but very different. Death magic is completely separate, but..." Levi bit his lip a moment, contemplating his words carefully. He raised his hand and turned it palm in, palm out. "It's a reflection. Separate and certainly not the same, but familiar enough to be confused for reality."

Levi glanced at Gypsy, but wouldn't hold her gaze. "Zombies are what happens when you try to extract an unwilling soul from the realm of death. The body may be healed, but the mind and soul will remain tethered by a magic that is far too powerful to break." His eyes settled on Cori. "It is possible to bring someone back from the dead, but it must be achieved by natural and magical means very near the time of death."

Cori frowned. "What do you mean, natural and magical?"

"I mean that the body must be healed of the damage and then the magic can assist in recovering them. If the body is damaged, the soul will never voluntarily return. That would be like asking any of us to walk into a fire."

"Been there, done that," Gypsy volunteered. Cori got the sense that she was saying it as a joke, but it was likely true.

"While this is all very interesting, I do not think any of us has the skill to perform a voodoo ritual," Leona pointed out.

"What do mean I just stopped time?" Gypsy flexed her biceps. "I've got enough dark magic running through me for ten more rounds."

Leona scoffed. "Haven't you been listening, Grace? Dark magic is a contrary magic to death magic." She leaned in a little closer to her. "They used to call it humane magic, you know. But then realized how destructive it was, so they just dropped the e." Leona turned to Cori. "When he says that the magic is separate, that means that humans can't access it. And you." Leona turned her hardened gaze on Levi, but then she softened and spoke more gently to him.

"Don't get too caught up in the aspirations of your former mistress. She was not as powerful as she pretended to be."

Levi's chest puffed, and he looked like he might say something to defend Annette. Leona waited patiently, allowing him the opportunity to snap at her, should he wish to. Either because he was too afraid or because he realized he had no defense; he swallowed his castigation.

"Let's just worry about my rings for now," Cori said and led the way down the back hall to the exit nearest the dragons.

"Since when are you afraid of zombies, Grace?" Leona asked as they trailed after her. There was a hint of amusement in her voice.

"Shut up. Everyone's afraid of zombies," Gypsy insisted.

Cori pushed out the back door of the prison and stepped into the northern yard of the compound. She instantly regretted not grabbing her coat, since the breeze had picked up. She looked back at the others as they joined her and huddled their arms around themselves.

"Merde!" Leona complained. "It's cold out here!"

"So how are we going to do this?" Cori asked Levi.

His face fell, and he glanced at all of them before answering. "I'm not really sure. I'm certain they won't allow us to interrupt them, so we are just going to have to... take it."

Gypsy leaned down and pulled a slender blade from her boot. She flipped it around and offered the hilt to

Cori. She stared at it, questioning why she had gotten volunteered for this dragon phlebotomy, but she was wearing the answer.

She took the knife and looked at the dragons cavorting around the grave of the only woman who might have been able to save her son. The woman Danato had killed to protect the world.

21

G YPSY CHARGED IN A full-court press, with no intention of letting the temperament of an overgrown lizard determine her success. She roared just as the beast lowed. She leaped off the ground and landed against the dragon's belly with a punch-worthy smack. The knife in her right hand buried into the creature's abdomen, and she smiled at the achievement.

Gypsy's pride washed away when a clawed paw batted her nearly thirty feet away from the wound she had created. She landed next to Cori—who was also flat on her back panting from her previous efforts to get a drop of blood from the dragons. They had been working on the task for nearly twenty minutes, but the moment they passed the invisible barrier of the magical circle, the dragons were alerted to their presence and defended themselves against the bloodletting. Even when they peacefully tried to coax them into compliance, the dragons violently struck back. Leaving Gypsy with the impression that they were not just defending their blood, but the sanctity of their magical ritual.

Cori's head lolled over to look at her as they both lay there wallowing in the common pain of a dragon smack down. Gypsy could sense a camaraderie of human frailty between them. They were not enemies at that moment. They were equals.

Equally pathetic.

"Did you get it?" Cori rasped.

Gypsy smiled. "Of course I got it." She rolled over, bringing the knife for Cori to see. They both stared at the clean silver steel with grievous disappointment. "Where the hell is the blood?"

Levi came into view above them. "Dragon skin is very thick. The first six inches beyond that is usually just blubber."

Gypsy grabbed a fistful of Levi's pants and yanked until he dropped onto the cold ground with them. "Listen, you little shit." She brandished her knife in his face. "You drop one more piece of hindsight information on my toes and I will cut your vocal cords."

"Oh, leave the boy alone, Grace. He's already terrified of you."

"I'm not terrified," Levi defended.

Gypsy pressed her knife into his throat. "You should be." Despite the blade putting a slight rent in his neck, he didn't flinch or hiss with pain. Gypsy smiled at the subdued anger on his face that was masking the fear he was denying. "Mmm, looks like you have a history of pain, don't you?"

His eyes flickered over her face as they began to water. This rare show of vulnerability intrigued Gypsy. Normally she had no interest in the complex emotions of anyone, but for some reason Levi's pain made her thirsty for more.

"Gypsy, stop." Cori stood up and dusted herself off. When Gypsy didn't move, she leveled a hard stare at her. "He's just trying to help us." As much as Gypsy wanted to keep playing with her food, she knew that abiding by Cori's orders was going to be an important part of her future work. Not that she had any specific issue with taking orders from a woman, but she still wasn't sure that Cori was worthy of the esteem she had received so far in her career.

Clearly, Cori was a badass in her own right. Anyone willing to face down Frederique could earn that badge of honor. And yet now, she seemed disinterested. She seemed cold and empty. Could it be that the stress of this world had finally broken her?

Made her... weak?

Gypsy released her prey and stood up. She looked at the knife and then back at the dragon.

"What do we do now?" Levi asked, swiftly wiping his face as if he only had something in his eyes and was not brought to tears by Gypsy's threat.

"We don't do anything." Gypsy threw her knife at Leona, and the blade bounced off her thigh. "She does."

"Grace!" The fem-wolf stared down at where the blade had hit her leg. "These are not Hanes Her Way stockings, you psychotic bitch. I paid $200 for these." She fiddled with the rent in her pantyhose, trying to press the material back together as if it might magically fuse.

"Time to get off the bench, Princess," Gypsy scolded. "Go get us some blood."

Leona scoffed. "I am not going to wrestle with a dragon."

"Are you saying you aren't going to help Cori get her son back?"

Leona froze and looked at Cori as if she had just been caught in a lie. "That's not what I'm saying." Gypsy motioned for her to head over and take a stab at it—literally. Leona fidgeted as she looked at the dragons. "We don't even know if these rings will help the child."

"We don't know that they won't," Gypsy said.

"The rings allowed me to keep my memories during my wish relocation. They must have some immunity to the genie's power," Cori explained.

"That is unlikely. Ethan is an amateur spellcaster at best."

Cori glanced at Levi to see if he might have a different opinion on this subject. She hadn't had a chance to ask him if he knew about Ethan's mage status. Surely if Annette hadn't known, he wouldn't have. "That may be, but I have to try something," Cori defended, though it was clear to all of them that this was still a long shot.

Leona looked at the dragons but didn't move.

"Are you... afraid of the dragons?" Gypsy asked.

"What?" Leona blinked dumbfounded. "No!"

"Oh, Cori, listen to that. I think we just found Leona's weakness. Dragons make her nervous."

"I am a werewolf. I am not afraid of anything. Not even zombies. It's just... I'm..." Leona mumbled something that Gypsy didn't hear.

"You're what?" She leaned in to listen.

Leona rolled her eyes. "I'm allergic," she said louder.

Gypsy's mouth dropped as she stared at the wretched look of embarrassment on the fem-wolf's face. Cori also stared in shock at this revelation. Levi was eventually the first to release a chuckle. After that, they all had a good laugh at Leona's expense.

"Oh, very funny."

"Aside from the obvious fun that I am going to have with that later, I'm gonna need you to sneeze your way over to one of those things and get some blood."

"It's actually a rather severe reaction," Leona reluctantly admitted. Gypsy didn't balk at the statement. "I could die!"

"Yeah?" Gypsy gave her a cold as-death stare. "Just like we could have died getting bucked like rodeo clowns. Crown up, Princess, or get off the throne."

Leona scoffed and looked at Cori, but she was unlikely to have sympathy for her potential anaphylactic shock. She turned her attention back to the dragons, no doubt considering how to get the blood with minimal contact. Her dismal expression brightened, and she gleamed with renewed smugness. "I don't think you will need me to endanger myself after all."

"Oh, I think I will." Gypsy took a step closer, more than ready to stretch the definition of her obligations to protect Cori.

"There is another way to get the magical infusion."

"What other way?" Cori asked.

"Something besides blood and saliva." Leona lifted her hand and wiggled a manicured fingernail behind them.

Gypsy turned around and looked toward the dragons. Nothing had changed except that one of them was squatting down on her haunches taking the largest crap she had ever seen.

"Dragons are such mystical creatures," Leona said with mock reverence. "Everything they excrete is just dripping with magical energy."

Gypsy let out a soft chuckle and then frowned. "Will that work?" She turned the question to Levi.

He nodded. "As long as it's fresh."

Leona moved over to him and rested her arm gently over his shoulder. "It's still steaming, sweetheart. It doesn't get any fresher than that."

Gypsy looked at Cori, who was reasonably horrified by the task ahead of her. Gypsy gave her a small salute and retrieved her knife before finding a good spot to watch the impending spectacle. As far as Gypsy was concerned, she was on a break from this shit.

22

GYPSY CRINGED AS SHE watched Cori dip her rings one by one into the pile of poop that was as tall as she was. She had to admit the woman was being a good sport about the undertaking. Determination breeds bravado. It wasn't until Cori started puking that Gypsy lost some respect for her. That seemed to be the way their relationship was panning out so far, though. Props to her results, just not as much for her poise.

"Eck," Leona groaned beside her. "I don't know how Danato does it?"

"Does what?"

"Run a prison that is part asylum and part farmyard." Leona sighed. "He's an admirable man to take on such a duty."

Gypsy blinked and turned to Leona. "Admirable?"

"You don't think so?"

"Ah, yeah, he's great. I've just never heard you speak so fondly about a human male before. And certainly not one that you aren't humping at the time, and even then you aren't usually talking about their work ethic."

"Well, maybe I have matured."

Gypsy scoffed, then frowned. "Are you sleeping with him?"

"No, don't be ridiculous."

"Good."

"Good?" Leona asked.

"Yeah, I'm not interested in sharing spit with you."

"Sharing spit?" Leona let out an elongated and unnecessary gasp. "Did you sleep with him? Cori is not going to like that."

Gypsy smirked and shook her head. "No, I tried to climb the mountain, but it was too steep for me."

"Oh."

"He made me breakfast afterward, though. So that's pretty close."

Leona eyed her carefully, mouth twisting as if she wanted to say something clever, but couldn't think of anything. "We had coffee together," she finally spat out as if they were competing for Danato's attention. Perhaps they were.

"He had coffee with you, or you were both drinking coffee at the same time?"

"We had a nice chat, actually."

"I thought Danato hated fem-wolves."

Leona snorted. "Men hate anything they can't control. Why do you think we seek out such young companions? Their hormones run their brains. They are too stupid to be afraid of us. Oh, but when they figure it out..." Leona's eyes glazed as if she were thinking of a specific incident.

"You can see it in their eyes. It's as if you are suddenly transformed into a monster—horns and all."

Gypsy noted the ire in her voice but didn't want to remain on the subject since it wasn't likely to result in a conversation she wanted to have. "What did you and Danato talk about?"

Leona pinched her lips in thought. "Work. The burden of command."

Gypsy chuckled. "You poor bastards. How ever will you manage?"

"There is more to command than giving orders, Grace. Danato makes decisions every day that affect the lives of his prisoners and his employees. And I am deciding the fate of my entire species," Leona said more softly.

Gypsy didn't like the direction of this topic either, but she wanted to know more about Leona's change in character. She wondered if Cleos was stacking his deck and making her more open to unconventional ideas or if she had come across her altruism naturally. "Why the sudden concern about your decisions? I thought you were a take no shit kind of fem-wolf like your sister."

"I told you. I have matured."

"And what inspired that sudden maturity?"

Leona propped her hands on her hips. "Why should I tell you? So, you can mock me with it later?"

Gypsy raised her brow. "Well, I haven't matured, so yes." She smiled at Leona. She must have gotten the inflection right because Leona actually gave in and snickered at her humor.

The fem-wolf looked out at the dragons and lost all amusement on her face. "What do you think it's like for them? Living hundreds or possibly thousands of years. What would be the point? Especially like that."

"I'm not really good at philosophical debates, Leo."

"The life of a werewolf is designed to be short. My pregnancies have greatly extended my projected age, but still... I shouldn't be living much past 40. All of my decisions—what I eat, what I wear, who I fuck... It has all been based on the idea that I will not live to be an old woman. I embraced life as a constant death sentence."

"I presume all that changed when you started playing around with the hormone therapy."

Leona nodded. "Yes. The doctors are already predicting another ten years to be added to my life and potentially even twenty with additional therapies."

Gypsy considered this for a moment before contributing. "You aren't afraid of dying. You're afraid of living."

Leona turned to her. "Yes. What a spectacle I must be. A fem-wolf afraid of more time."

"Well, you should be afraid. Wrinkles, varicose veins, incontinence—you're gonna be a mess."

Leona nodded and put on a small smile. "I am not afraid of age. I am afraid of seeing the consequences of my actions. I am uprooting my people. Disconnecting them from their animal side. I don't know what that will do to us. Will we evolve or will we de-evolve? Perhaps someday I will be viewed as a hero instead of a harlot, but for now, I will only live long enough to witness the strife I have created."

Gypsy nodded, understanding her worries, but she had nothing to contribute. She wasn't a politician. She wasn't a scientist. She wasn't even a werewolf. She had no way of knowing the outcome. However, Cleos probably did? "Does Cleos support your choices?"

"Yes."

"Then don't worry about it. You're doing the right thing."

Leona glanced at him slightly confused. She seemed to enjoy the simplicity of her response—as if she hadn't thought to put her faith in the man who had been guiding them correctly so far. After a moment of silence, she walked away. "I'm hungry," she called back to Gypsy.

23

Cori sat next to Gypsy in the cafeteria, staring at the massive pile of food that Leona had brought over on her food tray. Instead of grabbing a slice of meat to fill one of the squares, she had taken an entire ham leg. "Are you really going to eat all that?" Cori asked delicately. There was no room to fat-shame a woman so slender, but she certainly didn't want an entire ham to be wasted if she took two bites and decided that she wasn't hungry anymore.

Leona looked up, drawing her tray closer as if Cori might steal her meal from her.

"You're kidding, right?" Gypsy asked. "You haven't seen a fem-wolf eat?"

Cori blinked at her, trying to remember a time when she had seen Leona eat, but she hadn't. A beverage, but not a meal.

"Well, you're in for a treat. Assuming you like train wrecks."

"Shut up, Grace. You are one to talk. You shovel your food in like an ill-mannered child."

"Yes, shovel, as in, with a fork and spoon, like a human being, with opposable thumbs." Gypsy flaunted her thumbs, rotating them dynamically.

"I am not unevolved. I am just hungry."

"You better get to it then; you're starting to drool." Gypsy motioned to the corner of her own mouth.

Cori had assumed that Gypsy was just giving her grief, but there was in fact a long steady dribble of saliva pouring from the corner of her lips, like a dog anticipating its meal. Leona wiped away the liquid and turned her sad puppy eyes to her ham. Cori got the sense that her animal side and human side were fighting each other. She wanted to maintain her image of civility, but she was obviously famished.

"Go ahead and eat, Leona. I won't—" Cori barely got the permission out before the woman dove her face into the meat teeth first. The display was so enthusiastic that Cori struggled not to laugh. She glanced at Gypsy, who was watching her amusement with a satisfied smirk.

When the humor of the moment lulled, Cori sat back in her chair and fiddled with her rings. Aside from the residual smell of feces—which she was certain would not wash off for days—there was no power emanating from them.

"No luck?" Gypsy asked.

Cori glanced at her and shook her head. "How did you know dragon poop would be a source of magic?" She asked Leona across from her.

Leona looked up from the ham bone she was gnawing on. "Everything the dragons create is magical," she said with a full mouth. "Blood, saliva, snot—it just gets grosser from there. Just ask your husband." Leona dove in for another bite of food. Cori heard a quiet growl as she ate—like a puppy fighting to keep control of its food supply.

"What happens when you kill one?" Gypsy asked abruptly.

Cori and Leona both gave her wary looks.

"Why would you ask that?" Levi asked from the next table over. There was plenty of room at their table since it seated six, but the young man seemed reluctant to sit between Cori and Gypsy—and judging by the noises coming from Leona he probably didn't consider proximity to the fem-wolf a safe option either.

"Just curious. I mean if that sorceress spilled out dark magic after her expiration then maybe I could plug a dragon and juice myself up to sorceress level." Gypsy raised her thumb and made a clicking sound with her tongue.

Cori could see that Levi was beside himself with fervor. Not only was Gypsy suggesting the very creation that Danato had eliminated by force not long ago. She was proposing the murder of an animal that was no doubt as sacred to him as it was to Annette. "She's kidding, Levi."

"Am I?" Gypsy asked.

Cori gave her an acidic look. "She likes to say things just to get a rise out of people."

Gypsy's lip curved up slightly. "I also like to *do* things to get a rise out of people." Gypsy slid her hand across the table and stroked the thin scar that circled her wrist. The only evidence of her formally separated appendage.

Cori took several heavy breaths trying to control her anger, but as usual, she wasn't very good at it. Gypsy's smile broadened, and Cori couldn't take it anymore. She ripped the chair out from between them and stood up. To her surprise, Gypsy didn't flinch at her action. Nor did she try to wriggle her arm free of the weight she pressed down on it, pinning it to the table.

"Mmm, there she is," Gypsy groaned almost carnally, which disgusted Cori even more.

"No one is going to kill a dragon. And the last thing we need is for you to be a superpowered sorceress. It's bad enough that you have any magic running through your veins." Gypsy clenched her jaw and her breathing increased to a pant. "Let alone—"

"Cori," Leona scolded her. "Enough!"

Cori couldn't understand why Leona was coming to the woman's defense until she saw Gypsy's glistening eyes release two perfect teardrops. Her jaw was tense with a restrained grimace. She wasn't crying out of sadness. This was pain.

Cori looked down at Gypsy's forearm. The flesh beneath was steaming—burning from the heat in her hands. She gasped and released her grip. A perfect red handprint remained in the flesh, moisture already glistening to the surface in an effort to repair the deep scald with a protective scab. Gypsy drew her trembling arm back and sniffed away the drainage brought on by her tears.

Cori looked at Leona. The fem-wolf looked unhappy about the incident, but she seemed to understand that Cori hadn't meant to be so cruel. She didn't even know the rings were working yet.

Cori turned to Gypsy with yet another level of annoyance added to the excessive pile that had already built up over the years. "You... You did that on purpose."

"Your emotions tend to set off the rings. I was just giving you a little push."

"You should have told me I was hurting you. I would have stopped."

Gypsy turned and looked at her with an emptiness that could only be described in psychiatric terms. "That's the difference between you and me. You aren't willing to make enemies to get what you want."

Leona dropped her bone and spoke through her mouthful of meat. "That is a bigger pile of shit than Cori just stuck her rings in."

Gypsy's brow dipped as she stared at the fem-wolf. "Don't talk with your mouth full, you disgusting mutt."

Leona slammed her hands down beside her food tray and forcefully swallowed her food. "You always think you are such a rebel. You will do anything, hurt anyone, kill anyone to get what you want, and it is bullshit."

"I'm pretty sure my resume speaks for itself."

"Yes, yes, but you are not the only dissident in this room, you... vainglorious bitch. Cori has been fighting the rules of this prison since she first arrived. All at the expense of her relationships. And look at me. I overthrew my sister to get control of the council. I not only hurt my friends and my family—I put a deep, unfillable hole in my heart. You insist that what you do is more injurious, but you are wrong because the people you hurt mean *nothing* to you. Try staring your own flesh and blood in the face and telling them that you are betraying their trust and love for a worthy cause." Leona wiped her face and hands with her napkin and tossed it down on her tray. "No, Grace Gypsum, I reject your assumption of superiority in the department of upheaval." She stood from her seat. "You are working under the advantage of a frigid heart. As far as I am concerned, any woman who can endure a pain in her heart so deep that it makes her chest ache and still fight on, is stronger than you." Leona turned on her heel and left.

Cori watched after her for a moment before sitting back down in her chair. She knew Leona wasn't actually trying to stick up for her. Truthfully, that speech had probably been percolating in the back of her mind for a while. But she was glad Leona had said it. Anyone willing to knock Gypsy down a peg was going to get a gold star from her. It was just odd for Leona to be on the receiving end of that star.

When no one said anything, Cori cleared her throat and nodded to Gypsy's arm. "We should get you back to the infirmary."

To her surprise, Gypsy didn't object. She had either been put in her place for the time being, or the burn hurt more than she wanted to admit. As severe as it was, Cori had to wonder if Gypsy was volunteering herself for Cori's unintentional revenge for cutting off her hand. As noble as that should have sounded, it was yet again Gypsy keeping control of the situation. Even Cori's revenge was being directed by the woman. She didn't like that. She had little control over her life right now. She should at least have a say in whom she hurts and how much.

24

GYPSY HADN'T WANTED TO admit to Cori that her arm hurt like hellfire on a warm day, but when Cori forced her to endure her untrained medical care, she finally gave up being tough. "Ouch!" Gypsy hissed, drawing her arm away from whatever Cori was trying to dab on her wound.

"Sorry," she grimaced and drew away. "I'm not very good at first aid."

Gypsy grabbed the bottle from her other hand. "Not this." She tossed it in the trash beside the exam table. "There should be something labeled burn-jel or alocane in one of those cupboards." She pointed to the cabinets tucked in the corner of the small room.

Cori rummaged through them and found the cream that she needed. Gypsy instructed her how to apply it and then the bandage to follow. After she was done, she frowned at Gypsy's arm.

"What is it?"

Cori looked at her. "I was just thinking if Daniel were alive. He would be able to fix you right up."

"Yeah, but he's not," Gypsy said succinctly, not wanting to dwell on the subject. Regardless of her lacking emotions, she was rather perturbed by Daniel's death. He was an invaluable asset—not just to her, but to everyone. His loss was going to be greatly felt—later even more than now. "Come on." Gypsy patted her on the back gruffly—the best she could do in place of a "thank you." She jumped off the table. "Let's get moving. We've lost an hour already."

Cori's head shot up to the clock, which, despite slowing significantly, was still clicking away. By Gypsy's estimates, they had only gained another two hours with her magical brakes. Now that Cori's rings were at least partially charged, they had to figure out a plan and activate it before that bald bastard showed up to collect on his debt.

They headed out of the exam room, past the nurse's station, and stepped through the shattered door. One of the nurses had already cleaned the glass fragments up. There was no telling what messes those women had to clean up on a daily basis.

They met up with Leona and Levi, who were coming around the bend from the animal enclosures. They both wore worried expressions on their faces. "You are going to want to see this," Leona said.

Gypsy didn't like it when Leona was uneasy. She may not have respected her—much, but she appreciated the level-headedness she brought to otherwise chaotic situations. Gypsy exchanged a glance with Cori before they followed them through the airlocks to the aquatic section.

Gypsy could have predicted the ostensibly frozen scene she saw when she walked through the door. The violent part of the day was just beginning. Up until now, Ethan had been playing a part—the part of Danato's successor, but with his flesh and blood on the line from both directions, he was bound to defend him with his life.

Gypsy walked through the stage of paused players. She stopped in front of Danato and observed the feral expression on his face, paired with tears of remorse—proof of the pains he held so close to his heart, but never quite let in. Gypsy wondered if the man even knew how much he hated himself. She could see it. She could feel it. Anger is always the worst veil for misery.

She turned her attention to Belus. The small man was clenching his jaw so tight, fighting off the moisture that was gathering in his eyes. He was doing his duty too. Standing by Danato's side to the very end—even though he didn't agree with most of his decisions. Had there been even a sliver of hope in the genie's laws, he would have clung to it for life and limb, but there was nothing. Not one word to indicate that they could protect the boy—only destroy him.

Gypsy turned to face the beach ball-sized blue orb that was barreling toward them. Even in extreme slow motion, the flux of the electrical ball was visible. It looked like a miniature lightning storm hanging between them. Various areas would spark, and like shattering glass, they would splinter out into tiny veins. Then those ends would trigger a new reaction, continuing the storm over and over again, maintaining the strength of whatever vigor Efrat had put into it.

She stepped around the globe, feeling the static energy lifting her hair as she did. She was curious whether she could disrupt or deflect the ball at this stage, or if the magic had fused it tightly enough to reach its intended target regardless of what she put in its path. Since magic was by definition an aberration of natural physics, she could not rely on her science lessons when it came to an elemental. They were special—even by Earth magic standards.

Behind the orb, Gypsy found its creator. Efrat had not thrown this attack with survival in mind. His outstretched hands were ushering the deadly bomb, while the snarl on his face demanded punishment. The strength coursing through the attack may have had nothing to do with the child he was defending. He could have just wanted to be rid of his shackles once and for all. Regardless of the reason, he had been recruited for the roles of hero and villain today.

Beside Efrat, Ethan had much the same expression as Danato—a mixture of anger and pain stemming from a choice that he should have never had to make. His shoulder was twisted back, holding his son's head as he cowered behind Daddy's leg. A witness to the carnage about to unfold in his name—or rather his lack of a name.

Though young, the boy would remember this in the days to come. It would likely be his first memory. The day his father ordered the death of his grandfather.

"Oh my god!" Cori put her hands over her face, trying not to bear witness to the murder playing out before her. "No, no, no." She paced between the standoff as if debating which side she was supposed to be on. There was no winning side at the moment, but there was definitely a losing side.

Cori reached out to touch the orb. Leona leaped forward and pulled her away. "Cori, no!"

"I just need to absorb some of the energy," Cori rationalized as if she might just collect a few strands of the 300 million volts rolling through the air.

"There is too much," Leona said.

"She's right," Gypsy agreed. "You just got those ring-a-dings working. Even if that ball doesn't zap you right into a coma—you won't be able to absorb all of it." Cori's mouth twisted as if she were calculating how much the rings had protected her in the past. "That's a kill shot, Cori," Gypsy stated in case she hadn't figured that out already.

"I can't just let them die!" Cori looked at Danato and Belus, less than ten feet from death.

"Can't you?" Gypsy asked, drawing a scowl from Cori.

"Of course, I can't."

Gypsy sighed and walked around Danato and Belus. "Come on, Cori. We all know those rings aren't going to do jack shit against that genie. You didn't retrieve them so you could fight him." Gypsy moved to Cori and leaned in over her shoulder to whisper in her ear. "You did it so you could fight Danato."

Cori whipped around to face her. They were nearly nose to nose, but neither of them backed away. "Fight him maybe, but not kill him."

"Is that how that was going to go down? You were going to have a nice nonlethal fight with a bear. No blood. No tears. No pain." Cori shook her head but didn't define what she was saying no to. Gypsy could see the glimmer of guilt in her eyes as if she were admitting to herself what she had been preparing for. "I get it," Gypsy whispered. "It's easy for me to say because I don't love him. Leona's right about me. I don't have the attachments that make these decisions so difficult. I'm a stone-cold bitch compared to you, but that's why you should listen to me."

Cori's eyes fluttered over Gypsy's face. It astonished her that the woman was still listening to her, but she suspected that Cori just needed a push. A little devil on her shoulder to convince her that between two lousy choices, there was always a slightly better one.

"And what I am saying is that... maybe this is for the best. You don't have to carry the guilt for this one." Gypsy motioned to Danato's imminent murderer. "Efrat just took care of the problem for you."

"The problem isn't taken care of," Leona objected. "The baby is still going to become the genie."

"The genie isn't threatening to kill him. Danato is," Gypsy argued.

"What use is saving a child if he will be taken over by another being? The boy she knew is effectively dead then, anyway."

"Maybe not."

"Maybe, maybe, maybe!" Leona marched up behind Cori, speaking to Gypsy over her shoulder—now playing the part of the good angel to Gypsy's red devil. "Why are you doing this, Grace? Why are you encouraging this? You're playing games with real lives here."

"I'm not playing games!" Gypsy resented the implication that she wasn't taking this situation seriously. "I'm giving her permission."

"Permission to murder a man whom she cares deeply for?"

"Permission to do what she knows is necessary to save her son!"

"Bullshit!" Leona grabbed Cori by the shoulder and twisted her around to face her. "Cori, if you are going to listen to advice, then listen to me. As a mother, I would hope that we have more in common than this sadist."

"Masochist," Gypsy corrected.

"I cannot imagine losing one of my children. It would devastate me... but... I know that I would not want my child to be responsible for the deaths of so many others. If I knew that I could prevent it. No matter how much it hurt. I would do it."

"Speaking of bullshit," Gypsy objected.

"How dare you!" Leona glared at her, nostrils flaring.

"Cori, she just said that she is a mother. She isn't thinking about you or your child right now. She is thinking about *her* children. She doesn't want your son to endanger her children."

"I meant what I said," Leona argued.

"Only because the gun isn't at your kid's head!"

"Maybe we should—" Levi said just behind her.

Gypsy yelped and turned her overly defensive grip to his throat. "Where the fuck did you come from?" She ground her words out before releasing his throat.

"I came in with you," Levi said, sounding every bit of the young man he was.

Gypsy leveled a pointed finger at him. "There is something about you I don't like."

Levi frowned. "The feeling is mutual," he grumbled and rubbed his neck. "I was just going to say that we don't have to make this decision right now. Why don't we take advantage of this time delay? We can change the outcome of this attack, which will give us time to discuss the risks presented by the genie." Levi looked at Gypsy. "If Danato is our primary concern, then we can lock him up or sedate him. Killing him is unnecessary."

Gypsy scoffed at that. It was true she hadn't considered that option, but it was also true that Danato was not likely to stay locked up in his own prison for long. He was just as determined as he was strong.

Levi looked at Leona. "We have to help Cori come to a conclusion that will satisfy her, not us. A good leader never allows their personal preferences to interfere with their duty." Leona's eyes darted to Cori and Gypsy before settling on the floor.

Finally, Levi turned to Cori, who had been quietly accepting everyone's advice like a sponge. "All the time in the world will not change the options before you. Hearts break just as deeply in slow motion as they do in fast forward. The only thing this magic has done is give you the ability to make this decision outside the influence of the others." Levi nodded toward the battle. The men were busy trying to kill each other, while Cori was stuck deciding the fate of her son and, by extension, the trajectory of every relationship in her life.

As Leona said, regardless of her choice, she was going to lose her son. She just had to decide to whom she was giving him.

A god.

Or an angel.

C ORI WATCHED LEONA LIFT Danato up like an oversized mannequin and place him slightly to the left of Efrat's attack. Then she moved Belus to the right, placing him carefully, so there wasn't any risk of him falling over when she let go. Although Cori was satisfied they would survive, she shook her head. "This isn't enough."

"They are clear." Leona crouched behind Belus, examining the ball over his shoulder, to make sure he wasn't in its path.

"No, I just mean, the minute Efrat knows he missed, he'll fire again. We need to do something to disrupt the fight completely. Something to distract them."

"I've got just the thing." Gypsy strode over to Efrat and fumbled with his pants before pulling them and his drawers down to his ankles. She backed away and admired the view of his naked form. "That distracts me."

Leona peeked around Gypsy and raised her brow in interest. "Is it certain his mate would be electrocuted?" she murmured to her.

"You wanna test the waters, be my guest."

"As amusing as that is," Cori interrupted their gawking. "I think it will take more than Efrat's dick to tamp out the tension in the room."

"Okay," Gypsy agreed and moved to Ethan.

"Gypsy!" Cori snapped.

Gypsy turned back. "Oh, come on, Cori, I bet he's got a prizefighter in there."

"Oh, he does," Leona drawled nostalgically. Cori turned an angry glare at her, and she immediately flustered. "Not that I've experienced it."

"Moving on to more appropriate distractions," Cori said as she moved to the tank nearest them. There was a merman perched against the glass, admiring the pretty blue lights outside. "I think we should use what's available to us." Cori tapped on the glass.

Gypsy nodded approvingly. "That'll be fun too." She sauntered over to the ladder against the back wall and rolled it to the tank. After locking it into place, she motioned to Leona with a lady's-first gesture.

"What?" Leona asked, baffled.

"Ah, you didn't think I was strong enough to pull this slippery merman out of there, did you?" Gypsy looked at Cori. "And I'm gonna guess that your rings don't absorb physical strength." Cori shook her head. "So, that leaves you, Princess."

Leona looked between them and even back at Levi, who was smartly staying out of the way. "I'm not touching that thing. It stinks."

"It smells like a fish, get over it," Gypsy insisted.

"No! Mermin secrete oils to keep predators away. It stinks like putrid food."

Gypsy moved closer to her. "Then maybe you should take your clothes off before you get wet." Gypsy went so far as to lift the hem of her skirt.

"Uck!" Leona batted her hands away. "You're so disgusting, Grace. Why must you make everything uncomfortable? You aren't even a lesbian."

"I could be for you." Gypsy pinched her butt as she retreated from her. Following that, she immediately ducked to avoid Leona's swinging backhand.

Despite the peril they were in, Cori found herself smiling at the interaction. It reminded her of Heaton and Daniel's banter. Unfortunately, that thought brought her right back to her current state of entanglement. "Please, Leona," Cori said, rather than insist.

Leona looked at her—pity filling her features. She waggled her head in frustration. "Oh, merde." She removed her clothes, leaving on her bra and panties, and climbed the ladder to the tank. "I want credit for this. You tell Danato I am being a good sport." Leona jumped into the tank, going so far as to plug her nose.

"Why does she all of a sudden care about Danato's approval?" Cori asked, remembering that she was also trying to be nicer at his request.

"I think she has a crush on him," Gypsy said without ceremony.

"What? But she's..." Cori was about to say something about the age difference between them, but considering the life span of werewolves that didn't really matter.

"I think she's getting tired of pubescent men—thick-headed on both ends."

"But why Danato?" Cori's face cringed, still unable to imagine the odd love match.

Gypsy smirked at her. "Take your daddy-glasses off, honey. Your boss is quite a catch. Given the chance, I would get a ticket for that ride too."

"Oh, please no," Cori murmured not half as much to Gypsy as to the man upstairs.

Before Gypsy could further sully Cori's image of Danato, Leona exploded from the water—jumping out rather than using the ladder. She landed on the floor in front of the tank with the merman in her grip. Once she was stable, she dropped him. The merman landed on the tile with a wet smack. "Uck!" Leona held her hands out from her sides, not wanting to touch anything additional on her body. "I will stink for days."

After setting the scene with enough confusion to prevent the attack from continuing, Leona washed herself off in the emergency shower station before redressing. Despite the rinse, however, she still smelled like rotting vegetables.

Gypsy whistled after they passed through the last airlock together. "Wow, you weren't kidding about that smell."

"I hate you," Leona said to Grace, though there wasn't much enthusiasm in her riposte. She seemed more harrowed by smelling bad than anything they had gone through so far.

"Between you and Cori's hands, I may have to invest in nose plugs."

Leona let out a screech, and Cori looked back to see if she was going to finally attack Gypsy. Instead, she found her cowering behind the woman, her hands pinched around her biceps.

"Oh, don't touch me, stinkpot." Gypsy squirmed out of her grip.

"What the hell was that?" Leona pointed ahead of them.

"What was what?" Cori searched the area for a predator or a significant anomaly.

"That!" Leona shrieked as something small zoomed across the floor ahead of them, darting between the extra or broken animal cages that lined the wall. "Is that a rat?"

"Oh... my... god." Gypsy stared at the woman over her shoulder. "I am so embarrassed for you right now."

"Shut up, Grace! It ran right over my foot. I hate rats."

Gypsy shook her head. "You're a werewolf," Gypsy enunciated the words for her. "There's about eighty monsters upstairs that could put you down with a single bite, and you squeal about a rat running past your feet."

"They carry disease!" Leona argued.

"We don't have rats," Cori objected. "At least not anymore."

"Everyone says they don't have rats until they see one," Leona said.

"It's not a rat," Levi announced. Cori noticed Gypsy jumped again. For some reason, she was having trouble remembering where he was—or that he was there at all. Granted, the young man walked softly, but he wasn't invisible. She was used to Ethan's light-footed approach, so rarely did anyone surprise her anymore. "We should leave."

"If it's not a rat. What is it?" Cori asked.

"Don't worry about it." Levi moved toward the entrance of the stairs, encouraging everyone to follow. Leona readily followed him. Gypsy walked on, but stopped when she noticed Cori lagging.

Cori debated following Levi's instructions. She respected his advice—more so than she should, since she really didn't know him that well. However, there was something reassuring about his words. As if he was packing years of experience into each statement he made. In many ways, Levi reminded her of Ethan at that age. He was mature beyond his years and unjustifiably confident in his actions. She assumed that, also like Ethan, Levi may have had a hard life to earn that maturity.

And yet, it was because of Cori's trust in Levi that she couldn't walk away. She already suspected that what had run across the floor was not a rat. Levi's encouragement for her to walk away merely added evidence to her suspicions.

Curiosity was not a trait to be encouraged in the world of the supernatural, but Cori, despite her common sense, shifted closer to the tiny creature that had taken refuge behind the equipment.

"Cori, don't," Levi insisted.

Cori stopped and looked at Levi. The worried look on his face confirmed her hypothesis. The slow, earnest shake of his head should have been reason enough not to move closer to the critter, but part of her knew that this would be her only opportunity to see it. The shift in time and movement was the only reason they knew it was there in the first place. On any other day, it would have been just a flicker on the edge of their vision. Something to pass off as her imagination so she didn't have to consider the possibility of a world that overlapped her own.

The conspiracy building between Levi and Cori alarmed Gypsy. She reached into one of her pockets and pulled out a switchblade. She popped it open before following Cori to peek behind the cage. Though Cori was certain that weapons were not a good idea, she didn't discourage her since the thumping of her heart was as much from fear as anticipation.

Cori kneeled down and peeked into the crevice between a line of metal bars and a brick wall. Instead of a rat, she saw a glowing creature not more than three inches tall. It wasn't quite flying, but rather hovering over the floor. Cori tried to focus on the features to determine if it looked more mammalian or bug-like, but it was too small to see well. It was mostly just bright.

"What the hell is that?" Gypsy asked, pressing in behind her to get a closer look.

"I think it's..." Cori trailed off in a stupefied trance.

"Is that a flippin' fairy?" Gypsy's voice held the same shocked awe that the moment deserved. No one, save but a few lucky or unlucky souls had ever witnessed such a being.

Cori glanced up at her, eyes glistening with cheerful tears, and nodded.

As she stared at the tiny flurry of light, Cori noticed two little red dots had appeared on it. It took a moment before she realized they were eyes. The feeling of intelligence and acknowledgment pierced her stupor. Almost instantly she switched from being an observer to being the observed.

"Don't look at it!" Levi yelled at them.

Despite the palpable sensation of mounting danger, Cori couldn't stop looking at the little thing. And for a split second, she could see the eyes clearly despite the distance. A flash of red, angry, feral eyes that could only belong to monsters. They were glowing brighter than the rest of it, blocking out the rest of the world. Images of Tinker Bell dissipated from her mind as she imagined a swarm of rabid wasps ready to attack with punishing little stings.

Cori couldn't move; the terror whittling away at her mind was making her freeze instead of run. She couldn't even close her eyes. Why hadn't she listened to Levi?

"Help them!" Levi yelled.

There was a growling groan, and a moment later, Cori was on her back beside Gypsy with Leona towering over them. The weight of her hands pressed against each of their chests, making it hard to breathe, but Cori was relieved to be away from the glowing red eyes that were bound to find their way into her nightmares despite the house's protection. "What is wrong with you two?" Leona looked at Cori, demanding that she take the bulk of the blame. "Didn't Danato warn you not to observe the fae?"

"Yeah, I've just never seen one before," Cori murmured. "I couldn't resist."

"Try harder." Leona helped them both back up with an easy tug.

"How can you have been in this prison for this long and not seen everything?" Gypsy asked Cori.

Cori looked back at her. "I've only ever seen glimpses, but never one standing still like that."

"Fae move too fast for anyone to see," Levi explained. "They must have slowed down with the spell."

Leona snorted. "The fae don't do anything they don't want to do. This one must be wounded or something."

"Then we should leave it alone," Levi suggested eagerly.

"I agree." Leona looked back in the creature's direction. "There is not enough strength or bravery in the world to compete with the fae."

"Oh, yeah." Gypsy crossed her arms.

"That was not meant to be a challenge, Grace. Sometimes it is not appropriate to poke the bear."

"I don't know; I've already poked a genie this week. I might as well go after a fairy."

"You did what?" Levi asked incredulously.

"Please do not make me put you in a headlock," Leona said. "You know how opposed I am to physical contact with you."

"Given that stench, I'm in agreement for once."

Leona's face pinched with pouty contempt. "This is twice now that I have helped you." Leona held up two fingers as she walked away. "Don't you forget it," she called back to them.

Cori started to follow but now Gypsy was the one hanging back to stare at the fairy. "I think they're right. We shouldn't complicate things."

Gypsy's mouth twisted in contemplation. "Yeah," she said. "We don't want to complicate things." Though Gypsy voluntarily walked away from the hiding fae, she sounded perturbed.

26

As Gypsy descended the stairs with the others, she got an uneasy feeling. She slowed her steps to a stop and waited on the landing for the echo of her footsteps to catch up with her. Cori reached the next landing before she looked back at her, bewildered by her lagging pace. "What is it?"

Gypsy shifted to the edge of the landing. "Something isn't right."

Cori looked at Levi and Leona, who were already down to the next flight. "What do you mean?"

Gypsy looked around and shook her head. "Don't you feel it? Don't you hear it?"

"Hear what?"

"The echo."

"Yeah, so." Cori shrugged.

"That isn't right."

"Nothing is *right* at the moment. You slowed down time."

"Yeah, sure, *I* did that, with little to no magical training or experience, cast a spell that slowed all of time to nearly a pause. Since when does human magic have that much control?"

"I can't explain it either, but it's irrelevant right now."

"Step back." Gypsy motioned for her to step back. Cori did so, moving against the wall. Gypsy backed up and vaulted over the steps and landed with a *bang in* the center of Cori's landing.

"What the hell, Gypsy?" Cori moved to leave, but Gypsy grabbed her shoulder. She gave her a fierce look, so Gypsy released her.

"Just wait, okay." Gypsy put a finger up and delicately climbed back up the steps. When she looked back, Cori had settled back into the wall, arms crossed and irked by her antics. Gypsy took a breath and with quick, heavy footfalls descended the stairs. Just as she reached Cori, the raucous of her footsteps arrived in double time, loud enough to make Cori plug her ears.

"Thank you for that," she said when the noise had subsided. "Like the time bubble isn't enough of a strain on my eardrums." Once again, Cori moved to leave.

"Corinthia," Gypsy hissed at her, making the woman freeze. She slowly turned to face her, with only half the anger she expected.

"I've asked you not to call me that."

"Yes, because your mother was the only person who ever called you by your given name. Which is probably why it draws your attention so easily. Some ingrained connection to being in trouble—like the way some mothers say the middle name."

"Thank you, Cleos." Cori rolled her eyes and turned around again.

"Seriously?" Gypsy threw up her hands. "Do I have to cut off another hand to get you to listen to me?"

"Oh, fine," Cori seethed and returned to the landing. "What?"

Gypsy motioned to the stairwell. "This isn't right—"

"I know."

"—because there shouldn't be a Doppler effect." Cori's face blanked and her eyes shifted downward, as if she were trying to remember her science lessons from high school. "Okay, you remember the train coming at you versus away from you. Choo-choo." Gypsy made a tugging motion with her hands. Something about her effort forced a snort from Cori, but she quickly pushed away any evidence of amusement.

"Yes, Gypsy, I remember trains."

"You know how a train coming at you compresses sound so that when it arrives, almost all the sound hits you at once." Cori nodded. "Okay, what does the train sound like going away from you?" Gypsy held up a finger and ran back up the stairs. There was the same warbling echo that they had been hearing in the stairwell, but Gypsy made it to the landing long before the sound stopped.

"Okay, I get it, but what does that have to do with us?"

Gypsy struggled to find the words. "Damn it. I hate the science crap." She joined Cori back on her landing. "If I froze time, then that means we are moving at regular speed and everything else is slow."

"Right."

"So why are our footsteps lagging behind us?"

"Because the world is—"

Gypsy stomped her foot, making another singular bang on the landing, which was not delayed. "Why not our voices?" Gypsy asked before Cori could get irritated again. Slowly but surely, her face shifted into a realized confusion.

"What are you suggesting has happened?"

"I don't think I slowed down time. I think I sped us up. That's why the footsteps follow us. We are moving faster than the speed of sound."

Cori considered that for a moment. "Okay, let's say it is the reverse. We are moving around super fast, and to us, everyone else is slow."

"Right," Gypsy confirmed.

"So the clock is moving at normal speed. We are just accomplishing more in a minute than we would be if we were moving normally."

"Right," Gypsy confirmed again.

Cori sighed and shook her head. "But it doesn't really change anything beyond the physics of sound movement."

"I agree; it doesn't change anything beyond the scope of the spell."

Cori stared at her blankly. Gypsy could tell she was frustrated as hell but was trying to be diplomatic and not scream at her for wasting her precious time. However, Gypsy didn't want to rush her to a conclusion. "I'm sorry; it's been a long night. What is your point?"

"I think we can agree it's more likely that I only affected the three of us with this spell and not the whole of time." Cori nodded. "So, if the scope of the spell has been reduced to us, then we have one very big question we need an answer to."

"And what is that?"

"Levi."

Cori shrugged. "He isn't affected by magic."

"Exactly." Gypsy smiled. "My spell could not have affected him. So why is he moving faster than the speed of sound, just like us?"

27

"WHAT IS THIS ABOUT?" Levi asked when Gypsy pushed him down into Danato's desk chair.

"Take it easy, Gypsy," Cori admonished her and propped herself against the desk opposite her so they could interrogate Levi together.

"I still don't see what the big deal is." Leona sat on one of the chairs ahead of the desk and propped her feet up on the other one.

"I am not explaining the Doppler effect to you again," Gypsy grumbled. "You are either with us or you can stay out of this."

"Fine," Leona stood, slapped a hand against Danato's desk, and leaned in to yell at Levi. "Tell us where the money is!" Leona perked her brow at Gypsy. "There, how was that?"

"Oh, thank you very much, 1940s mob boss. Just sit there and eat your chips."

Cori glanced back at the bag of corn chips pinched in Leona's far hand. "When did you get chips?"

"I stopped in the cafeteria when you two were talking on the stairs." Leona pulled out a handful to nibble on.

Despite it not being remotely close to lunchtime, Cori realized she was famished. Gypsy must have been feeling the same gnawing hunger because she reached out for the bag. Leona whipped it away, a slight growl emerging above the sound of her crunching.

"Hey!" Gypsy snapped. "Bad girl! No bite!"

"I am not a dog! Do not speak to me that way!"

"You snapped at me. That's what dogs do."

"I am a werewolf. I don't snap. I bite." Leona chomped her teeth together.

"You know what else werewolves do? They share."

"Not me."

"If you give us some of those chips," Cori interjected. "I'll tell you where Danato keeps a stash of his orange soap."

"Orange soap?" Leona asked between crunching.

"Gets out any smell—and I mean *any*."

Leona looked between the two women and tossed the bag of chips down on the desk. "Where?"

"Look in the bottom drawer of that file cabinet."

Leona dove for the file cabinet and ripped the drawer off its hinges to get to the orange bottle marked emergency use only. "Oh, merci!" She hugged the bottle and looked around for something.

"There's an emergency shower on the docks," Cori said.

Leona jumped up to leave but looked around the room. "Where did he go?" She pointed to Danato's chair.

"What?" Cori looked back and saw the empty chair.

"Son of a bitch!" Gypsy yelled and started looking under the desk in case he had just slipped down to cower.

"Was that door open before?" Cori asked, noticing that the office door was wide open.

"No." Gypsy rolled over the desk and ran out the door shouting in vain. "You can run, you little shit, but you can't hide!"

Leona looked at Cori. "She does not like losing."

"Yeah, but I'm not sure she knows how to play fair."

"I suppose I will have to stop her before she hurts him." Leona looked at the soap container longingly before placing it on the desk and following Gypsy down the hall. "Grace! You don't want to kill him! He is just a boy!"

Cori knew she should follow them, but she didn't have the energy. Everything was falling apart. She may have gained time, but it didn't do any good without a strategy. Perhaps it was just as simple as taking her son and running away. But she didn't know how long her speed would last, and regardless of her pace, a vehicle would still have a normal maximum speed. At this point, she could move faster than a horse. And with that in mind, could she safely carry her son with her while she ran faster than the speed of sound? Given the damage she had caused just by opening a door, what could she do to him if she moved him too quickly? Windburn? Gravitational pressure?

Cori sat in one of the chairs and leaned her face into her hands. She had no tears left to cry, and although she had just prevented Efrat from killing Danato, she was wondering if violence was now the best course of action. Like Gypsy said, he was the one trying to kill her son.

But what would become of her boy if the genie took him?

A monster?

A walking, talking God?

Was there even a difference?

The only thing certain was that he would no longer be her son.

"Cori."

Levi's voice made her jump. She looked at Danato's chair and saw him right where they had left him. He looked at her with the same piteous expression as everyone had over the course of the last 24 hours, but with the addition of the fear that Gypsy had put into him.

"Levi, what's going on? Where did you go?"

"I just phased out for a little while. I do that sometimes when I'm in danger or forgotten about."

"Forgotten about?"

"Yeah, people tend to forget about me. If I'm quiet and really still, they just stop seeing me."

Cori reached over and closed the door to Danato's office to block out Gypsy's ranting, which was still bleeding down the hallway. "Levi, what are you?"

"Nothing bad."

Cori gave him a small smile. "Of course not, but I thought you weren't magical."

"I'm not. I don't have any effect on magic."

"Then how can you just disappear?"

"I don't disappear; I just let light pass through me. I'm still technically here. I'm just not visible to your eyes."

"And how is that not magic?"

"Because my natural state is to be out of phase."

"You were born invisible?"

Levi looked at his lap, either embarrassed or frustrated; she couldn't tell. "It's complicated."

"It usually is. Gypsy's right, isn't she? Time hasn't slowed down. We are moving faster." Levi nodded. "How does that work for you? How are you moving fast if you can't be affected by magic?"

"It's complicated."

Cori realized Levi had no intention of explaining his secrets. She had spent far too many years working to unleash the secrets of the men around her. She wouldn't waste any more time digging for information that someone didn't readily trust her with. "Whatever?" Cori shifted to leave.

"Cori, wait. I'm not hiding anything from you. It's because of my magical immunity that I can pass through the world in a sort of phase space. Being invisible is my natural state because I don't technically belong here."

Cori shifted back in the chair again. "Where do you belong?"

Levi bit his lip nervously and glanced around. She got the sense that he was not supposed to be speaking about this to anyone. "I live... in between."

Cori narrowed her eyes on him. "In between what?"

He licked his lips and, before her very eyes, within the blink of an eye, he appeared beside her, holding her hand. She jumped but didn't scream. His touch was soft and eased her as quickly as his movement had alarmed her.

"I live between heartbeats." He reached out his hand and pressed it to her breastbone. There was nothing sexual about the contact, but even if there had been, Cori wouldn't have moved. She was feeling something coming from Levi that was undeniably harmonious. "I hide in the strands of light." Cori watched his face change from the handsome young man she knew to a long glowing elvish face. It was still Levi, but a more celestial version of him. "I dance between the raindrops, and if I run fast enough, I can even outrun time."

Cori felt the world around her fall away, and for a moment she was without bearings or conscious thought. All that surrounded her was light, light, and more light. What should have been abrading to her eyes was suddenly a long-awaited breath. She turned to look at this new world. She was floating as if she were underwater, but there was plenty of air. Warm and cool, it brushed against her skin as if she could feel each molecule, one at a time.

She reached out to touch the blur next to her, and her fingers went through it as if there was nothing there at all.

She reached out to Levi and found that he was solid. He was there—inside this world with her. Nothing else was real, but she was, and he was.

It was at that moment she knew she didn't belong wherever he had taken her. Be it the great beyond or the between as he described it, this was not a place meant for humans. This was a place for ghosts, angels, and—

The door slammed open, banging against the back wall, and Cori was instantly back in the real world staring at Levi. Gypsy's arms reached to Levi, pulling him out of the chair and taking his contact from Cori. She felt momentarily bereft and empty. She reached out for Levi like a life preserver, and he even reached back for her, but there was no escaping Gypsy.

"You little twerp." Gypsy slammed him into the far wall.

"How did he get past us?" Leona asked as she trailed in.

"No," Cori uttered as she slipped off her chair and sank to the floor, heavy with gravity. Even the air felt heavy on her lungs, as if she were breathing water.

"Let go of me!" Levi shouted and reached out for her.

Cori felt something cold ease up alongside her. She looked back to see who was trying to pick her up, but the arm scooping under her torso was not really there.

"What is wrong with you?" Leona asked. "Are you sick? Did he do something to you?"

"I don't know." Cori felt another weight on her. The body of the arm that was wrapped around her was now resting on top of her. She was being constricted and pressed, making her breathing even harder.

"Get off me!" Levi screamed in Gypsy's face as he struggled to get free. "I have to help her!"

"Levi," Cori breathed his name with her last remaining air, and then she heard it. Something that no living being should ever hear. A sort of cracking sound, like the joints of a spine cracking from top to tail, except it wasn't her spine.

The floor slipped from beneath her, and she was dragged away, but not before Levi freed himself from Gypsy and dove for her. He held her hand, tethering her to where she belonged, and though her body had not moved beyond falling flat against the floor, she was floating somewhere below it. As if someone had smeared her across the canvas of the world. But instead of spreading across the blank white space that Levi had shown her, she was off the edge of the frame, dangling in the unknown.

She heard a song, and she turned to look into the darkness that frightened her more than any monster she had ever faced. Someone was singing, but the words were unclear. She searched for a face, but there was nothing beyond pure, unadulterated darkness.

Levi yelled her name, and she looked forward again. He was straining to pull her back—it was a tenuous tug of war, and she was making it harder. She focused on his hand and imagined herself returning to him.

He yanked her back up, and she was forward, away from that netherworld and away from the floor. Her rise lasted only a moment before she collapsed again, this time landing on top of Levi and safely back in her right body—in her right reality. She listened to Levi's laborious breathing as she shivered against him—seeking more warmth than he had to give her.

"What the fuck just happened to you?" Gypsy paced around the pair of them—as angry at her lack of knowledge as any event that she had witnessed. "What did he do to you?"

"I'm sorry, I'm sorry, I'm sorry," Levi repeated—though not to Gypsy. "I just wanted you to understand."

"Understand what?" Gypsy asked.

Cori shifted to look at Leona, who was not as angry as Gypsy, but definitely suspicious of the activities that they had missed in their absence. "I'm so cold," she whispered through her chattering teeth.

Leona's face went slack, and she glanced at Gypsy before clearing her throat. "I—"

"Please," Cori added, unable to accept no for an answer.

Leona's shoulders sank, and she waved Cori to stand. "I am beginning to feel like a stand-in for your husband—lift this, hold this, warm my feet." Cori pressed into the woman's body, and she flinched. "Oh, you are cold. Come, come, everyone."

"Seriously?" Gypsy perked a brow.

"Feel her," Leona said with threat.

Gypsy slapped the back of her hand against Cori's neck and frowned. "Christ, she is cold. Levi, what the fuck did you do to her?" To Cori's surprise and appreciation, Gypsy pressed into her back, giving her a backward hug. She even rubbed her arms a little. Almost immediately, Cori felt better. As if the ice inside of her was thawing out.

"She rebounded," Levi said. "You interrupted me. She..." Levi snapped his fingers. "...landed too hard and lost her footing."

Cori looked at Levi, question after question adding to the ones already in her head. She wanted to ask where she had just been, but she already knew the answer. She would pretend she didn't and lie to herself as often as needed to maintain that ignorance, but she knew exactly where she had been.

And she never wanted to go back.

28

"**I** DON'T LIKE YOU," Gypsy said flatly as she stared across the table at Levi. They were back in the cafeteria so Cori could warm herself up with a cup of hot coffee. The woman looked positively traumatized after her *experience*. She was still shivering, giving Gypsy the impression that her temperature was not what was truly wrong with her.

Despite several death threats and a slew of cursing tirades, neither Cori nor Levi could give her an answer about what just happened. They had only been alone for a few minutes, but it was long enough for something to go wrong. Something bad.

Levi peered up at her from beneath his brow. His head had been bowed in shame since she had started yelling at him. He held her gaze long enough to say his piece. "You've made that abundantly clear. And the feeling is mutual." His gaze wilted as hers lit with ire. She rose, but Leona grabbed her wrist. Her bony fingers dug in but didn't pull her back. However, it would only take a small tug to bring her back down—so instead, she *chose* to sit.

"Enough with this rant, Grace. They obviously do not want us to know what happened."

Gypsy glanced at Cori, wondering if this was the case. The woman looked back at her with the same expression she had when she was begging for warmth—like she was standing on a bridge searching for one single reason not to jump off it. Levi had insisted that he could warm Cori back up again, but the poor woman was too frightened of him to let him near her. As it was, she had crammed her seat closer to the wall to get more distance between them than the additional chair.

"I told you; I didn't do that to her. You interrupted me, and she just—"

"Yes, but what did we interrupt!" Gypsy smacked her hand on the table, making everyone, including Leona, jump. "What did you do to Cori to turn her into a goddamn zombie!"

Cori seemed to rouse at the accusation but did nothing to defend herself. She just found a new point of nothingness behind Gypsy to stare at.

"You wouldn't understand. I just wanted to show Cori that she…"

"That she doesn't have to be afraid of you?" Gypsy stood and shifted away from the table before Leona could grab her. "Do we have an explanation for your ability to move through time faster than everyone else?"

"It doesn't matter," Cori said. She set down her coffee and pushed away from the table. She looked suddenly energized. "How much time do we have before..." Cori looked at the clock on the wall. Despite time moving slower, the deadline for the genie's acquisition was down to minutes. Levi had theorized that the spell would break once the Genie returned regardless of whatever magic Gypsy possessed. "Everyone upstairs now."

"You sound like you have a plan." Gypsy felt relief wash over her. She wasn't sure what Levi had done to her, but if it had helped wake her up, she would have to consider it a good thing.

Cori stared at her and took a slow breath. "Not a good one."

"Mmm, sounds promising."

Gypsy followed Cori out with Levi and Leona just behind them. They ran up the stairs silently, but the clamor of their steps soon followed them out of the stairwell onto the second floor. They ran to the section where Danato and the others were. A new battle had risen in the wake of their absence. Efrat had created an electromagnetic force field around Cori's son, blocking anyone from getting to him. Ethan and Danato were wrapped up in each other's clenched fists. Ethan's face was fierce and ready to shove Danato, but his mentor had already gotten the upper hand and was lifting him off the floor.

Gypsy couldn't help but stare at the power between the two men. Watching this battle in slow motion was beautiful to her. Their brazenness had been photographed in 3D. Their brawny muscles frozen like a living sculpture.

"Leona, help me." Cori moved to Efrat and placed her hand tentatively on his forearm. She looked up at the elemental as if he might be able to see her there. Perhaps he could, but it would only be for a second. Nothing more than a hallucination if he even recognized what he saw.

"What do you want me to do?"

"Get the baby."

"From in there?" She gaped at the wall of prickling energy that, even in slow motion, looked painful.

"I'm going to try to leech off as much power as I can. Then you get the baby out. You're the only one who stands a chance against Efrat's power."

"You do realize this is going to hurt a lot."

Cori sighed and rested her forehead against Efrat's chest. "Are you saying no?" she asked.

Leona glanced back at Gypsy as if she might help her get out of the obligations that came with her strength. Gypsy crossed her arms and perked a brow, effectively pointing her back to the bed she made for herself with her ego and birthright.

"Of course not," Leona snapped. "I was just preparing you for what may turn out to be a lot of screaming."

Cori nodded. "I'm sorry."

Leona moved up to the field and looked over at her again. "What are you going to do when you get him out?"

Cori looked at her, a certain determination overshadowing her sorrow. "I'm going to do my job." There was a pause as the women exchanged a look of worry before proceeding to free the child. Gypsy wasn't sure if the job Cori was referring to was as the pseudo-warden of this prison or as a mother, but either way, this plan started with getting past Efrat Alston.

Cori winced as her hands hit Efrat's scar—the mark of where his humanity ended and his elemental hands began. The rings glowed, and Cori groaned. Gypsy shifted forward, drawn by her desire to fix whatever was going wrong. Levi touched her shoulder, and she turned—hiding her surprise better than she had been.

"I think I can help her," he said. For a moment, she didn't understand why he was still standing there, but then she realized he was asking for her permission. He obviously didn't want her to tackle him the moment he got near her.

Gypsy rolled her jaw, still trying to pinpoint what it was about this young man that pissed her off so much. Maybe that was the point. Nothing about him pissed her off—and that in and of itself was so rare, she didn't know what to do with it. "Well, quit gawkin' and get to work."

Levi's mouth ticked up a bit, and he ran to Cori's aid. He stopped behind her and leaned in to whisper to her. Cori nodded, and he pressed closer against her. Gypsy smiled as the boy tried to lean into her without pressing his pelvis against her. Eventually, he relaxed into the reverse embrace—ignoring how it looked from an outside perspective.

Levi's fingers crawled up Cori's hand, much as hers had Efrat's. Unaffected by the snapping electricity from the elemental, he pressed his fingers over hers. He reached down and did the same to her free hand, lacing his fingers between hers. He leaned in close to her ear, and this time Gypsy heard his words. "Don't let go until I release you."

Cori took a breath and slid her hand, and Levi's, up a little higher, dipping directly into the magical field that Efrat was producing. A bright flash of light made Gypsy fall back. The blue mixed with yellow became a laser show, and then the field opened like a parted curtain.

Leona threw a "WTF" look at Gypsy before jumping into the field to grab the boy. She lifted him carefully and stepped back through with him.

Levi drew back on Cori, pulling her away from Efrat. Once they were away, she did as instructed, letting him release his grasp on her before she moved away from him. Cori chuckled as she turned to face him. He stared at her, confused. "What is it?"

She smirked at him. "You tickle. Why do you tickle?"

Levi's face went red, and he looked away. "I don't know." He shrugged. "Some people react differently to me than others." Levi glanced at Gypsy as if to include her in the odd reaction category.

Despite the innocence of this interaction between Levi and Cori, Gypsy didn't like it. Something had happened while she was out of that office—something very important—and she had missed it. Suddenly, Levi wasn't just a calm presence in a room full of raging idiots. He was now a force—a benign one or not—he was not the magical eunuch he purported to be.

Cori looked at her son and, much as Leona had, she picked him up slowly and carefully so she didn't abrade him with a rubbing touch or puncture his skin with an urgent reach. She looked over his face, her eyes on the verge of tears, but with a firm voice said, "You are my son. And you will always be my son."

The words compelled everyone to look at their feet as if they didn't want to inadvertently give away a secret. Gypsy admired Cori's stalwart approach to her motherly claim, but she was wrong. The genie would forever change her son and the world they lived in.

"And I will always love you."

At that moment, Gypsy couldn't help but picture the world overrun by a bad episode of "I Dream of Genie." The thought prompted an immediate snort of amusement.

Everyone looked at her—equally baffled and aggravated by her inappropriate outburst. Leona mouthed something along the lines of, "*What is wrong with you?*" Gypsy considered explaining her thoughts or apologizing, but the benefit of being her was that she didn't have to justify anything she did. Nobody expected much from a sociopath.

Gypsy risked looking at Cori to see how angry she was, but most of her attitude had subsided. She was just looking at her, like an odd child destined to be stuck sitting alone in the lunchroom. At the very least, Gypsy offered her a grimace to assure her she was not trying to provoke her.

Cori turned her attention to Leona and Levi. "I need you two to stay here. If the spell breaks before I return, make sure they don't kill each other." Cori nodded to Danato and Ethan, already on the verge of self-destruction. She frowned at the display and then turned to leave.

"Where are you going?" Leona asked.

"Gypsy and I have some work to do."

Gypsy looked at Leona's baffled face and shrugged. Cori had not updated either of them on her. However, since Cori was taking the lead and they had very little time left, Gypsy wasn't about to argue with the only active effort the woman had made since her arrival.

29

G YPSY HAD NO MEMORIES of the old layout of the top floor—at least none of her own, but the transformation from battle zone to laboratory museum was impressive. Everything in the prison, barring the basement, was shiny white and glossy, but this floor had a slight gray tinge. Mostly because they specially designed the lighting for Cleos's photophobic constitution, but also because the floor was painted concrete instead of large tiles. The walls were drywall instead of painted blocks. Since there was no longer any concern about prisoners escaping, the board had opted to build proper walls that allowed for enclosed electrical lines as well as providing structure for hanging equipment and cabinets.

As Gypsy looked around, she noticed how small the space looked with all the display cases and workstations. There was still a good portion of the floor beyond the next section that was a wasteland of supplies, but it was all to prepare for Cleos's expansion. Should he ever meet his primary objective of saving the prison, he would begin to hunt for more profit. Because there was always room for more profit.

Gypsy smiled as they neared the pedestal that held the genie's lamp. She was looking forward to a second round with her favorite demi-god, but Cori bypassed the artifact and stopped at a row of file cabinets with short, wide drawers.

"Aren't we going to have a chat with Mr. Clean?"

"No," Cori said quietly. "The time for negotiating is over." She opened the first drawer of the cabinet and scanned the carefully bagged and tagged small objects that lined the green felt interior.

While the case was likely designed for jewelry, there were only a few rings in the mix. Most of the objects were fairly uninteresting—fish hooks, marbles, teeth. There were coins that looked old enough to be worth money, but most of them bore a very distinct skull and crossbones symbol on their labels—signifying to even the slowest learner that money could not buy happiness. Gypsy reached out to examine a particularly shiny silver thimble, but Cori slapped her hand and closed the drawer.

In the next drawer were some slightly larger objects—silverware, compacts, pens. Cori slammed the drawer and moved to the next drawer—knobs, hinges, screwdrivers, and a dead rat. Gypsy leaned in to read the label—desperate to know why the dead rat was important, but Cori was already closing the drawer. She was frustrated that she wasn't finding what she needed. Rather than continue searching the drawers, she grabbed the three-ring binder from the top of the cabinet and resorted to reading the logs.

Cori scanned the entries that had been painstakingly created the last time Gypsy was here. If there was anything good that had come from that day, it was avoiding the tail end of that garage sale. She still had nightmares about being gored by an elephant. She wasn't sure if that was normal following an interaction with the bone sword, or just specific to her morbid personality, but she was very aware of how close she was to the weapon. It was calling to her from the glass case mounted on the wall behind her. She rubbed her fingers together rhythmically, trying to calm her desire to touch it. She wondered if a normal person might succumb to the desire more readily or if the promise of death was enough to frighten them away.

Rather than go after the sword, she pulled out a pack of cigarettes and lit one. Cori glanced up at the sound of her lighter. She frowned and then looked over at her son. She probably wanted to remind her about the effects of secondhand smoke, but given the time variables in play, she would be done with it before the boy had taken in his second breath. Regardless, Gypsy pointed her exhalations to the ceiling. She watched the smoke billow out of her mouth with the force of her lungs only to linger in a cloud above her, slowed by the pressure of real-time.

"What are you looking for?" She finally asked. Cori continued to search without answering her. "I'm just saying, I can read. In case that wasn't listed among my talents."

"Do you like me?" Cori asked, not looking up.

Gypsy snorted and barked a laugh. "I'm sorry, what?"

Cori tossed the binder on top of the file cabinet and moved down to the next one. She grabbed that one and started searching for it in the same fashion—with a dragging finger and flickering eyes. "I just can't figure out whether I like you. I mean, I guess I have to respect you and, God help me, I think I'm even starting to trust you, but…" Cori looked up. "I don't know if I like you."

Gypsy moved forward and leaned on the cabinet Cori had just given up on. "You know it's not necessary, right? Liking me. We can work together and hate each other, just so long as we respect each other. Hell, look at Leona and I. I hate her guts, but I'm still gonna watch her back."

"Maybe that's what I should be asking, then. Do you respect me?" Gypsy pinched back her smile as best she could, and Cori frowned. "You don't, do you?"

Gypsy shook her head. "I didn't say that. I'm just very amused at your timing." Gypsy motioned to the clock on the wall, which was now only a few minutes from returning to real time.

"Tell me what you really think of me, Gypsy."

Gypsy bit her lip back and shook her head. "Why do you want to know?"

Cori reached into the second drawer and pulled out a long white box. She slipped the box into her back pocket before Gypsy could read the number on it. "Because I'm about to ask the biggest favor I have ever asked in all my life, and I want to know if I'm asking you as a friend or if I should expect to be indebted to you."

Gypsy propped her hands on her hips. "I'm not into games, Cori. What's this about?"

"When I lost the rings..." Cori lifted her hand, staring at the rings that seemed to be active again. "I felt useless. I felt like I didn't belong here. I felt angry, and I wanted to make up for it by being impetuous and resistant. It was the only way I knew how to behave when my life was beyond my control. Then Duke. Then Daniel. Then... this. That's when it hit me. I have no control. I never did. I have choices and decisions. And none of them will give me what I truly want. I will never have a normal life... and neither will my son."

Gypsy glanced at the little boy and then moved closer to Cori. "Why are we up here, Cori?"

"That's what it means to be the warden of this place. To give up all expectations of your future. To surrender your fantasies and focus on what's right in front of you."

Gypsy frowned at her. "It sounds like you've made a decision."

"I thought it was about choosing sides. I thought it was about choosing my son or choosing the world. It's not." Cori's eyes were watering, but she wasn't truly crying—it was just in the background. The scenery along the side of the road of their conversation. "It's about doing the right thing. It's about accepting the facts instead of praying for a miracle. The child must be of warm flesh and no name. I cannot give him a name, so I have to make his blood cold."

Gypsy took a breath, not entirely certain of how to handle this situation. For a moment, she wondered why Cori hadn't asked Leona to come with her—to have another mother comfort her in this moment. But perhaps a shoulder to cry on was not what Cori wanted.

Gypsy took a step back, but Cori reached out and grabbed her arm. Gypsy glanced at the contact and immediately felt her defenses rise as if the woman were about to punch her. Though it wouldn't be a fist, it would indeed be a hit. One she wasn't entirely sure she could recover from. She stared back at the woman's earnest and pleading eyes as she spoke the words that struck more fear in her than a genie or a fairy.

"Gypsy, I need you to kill my son."

30

G YPSY WOULD HAVE SLAPPED her if she hadn't still been holding her son. "Do you even know what you are asking?" She flicked her cigarette off to a safe corner to die out.

"I'm asking you to do something a mother shouldn't be required to do."

Gypsy laughed. "Yeah." She continued to chuckle as she labored through a deep breath. "I have rules. I can't violate those rules."

"Rules?" Cori shifted and carefully set her son on the floor before moving closer to Gypsy. "The only rules you have right now were given to you by Cleos. He told you to protect me. Well, this is what I need protection from."

"If you're just going to kill him, then let Danato do it!"

"No!"

"Why not?"

"Because I don't want him to live with that memory. This is my decision. I will carry it out."

"You mean I will carry it out." Gypsy could feel her body shake with the anxiety of violating her last true rule.

The barrier between her and her humanity. She couldn't do it, even if it meant going against Cleos's mandate.

"I need you to do it for me."

"Why?"

"Because I'm afraid I'll miss!" Cori yelled even as her hands reached out and clasped onto her shoulders. Gypsy wanted to throw her off and run, but she hated looking weak even at this moment. "You have training as a nurse. You can do this for me. I can trust you to make it quick."

Gypsy shook her head. She backed away but only got as far as a heavy stone pedestal. She pressed her back against it, feeling the weight against her and on her all at once. She slid down the rock until she was sitting on the floor. "You don't know what you are asking?"

Cori's features went cold. She released Gypsy and stood upright. "None of this would be necessary if it weren't for you. You know that. I had a solution to my wish reality. All I had to do was agree to the conditions, but you screwed it up."

"That wasn't me!" Gypsy defended.

"The hell it wasn't," Cori yelled back. "You and I both know you are just a temper tantrum away from being her." She kneeled down and analyzed her like a bug. This was no longer the woman Gypsy knew. This was the woman who had stood up to Frederique. It was true everyone possessed a dark side, but since Cori's was so rare, Gypsy couldn't help but be impressed by how much it looked like her own reflection. "I think you do your best to play this part—the devil-may-care sidekick and occasional hero, but that doesn't mean you are a good guy."

Gypsy shook her head, resenting that she could never do enough to prove to Cori that she would not snap and kill everyone she loved. Ironic since Cori was only bullying her now because she was refusing to kill someone she loved.

"All of this is your fault, Gypsy. It may not have been by your hand, but it was your psychopathic tendencies. The fact that you exist—that your proclivities exist—is why I am being forced to execute my son to save the people that I love from a horrific decision." Cori stood and lorded her height once again. "I asked you whether I would be requesting this as your friend or if I would be in your debt, but the truth is you already owe me this favor. You owe it to me to fix this. You need to do this to make it right once and for all."

Gypsy looked at the child and felt a swell of dark magic inside her. The voices of a thousand mothers were already wailing their tales of woe. Soon they would break through, and she would not be able to plug her ears to stop her mind from hearing them. "This will be my undoing," she whispered mostly to herself.

"I don't care." The hard edge in Cori's voice sent shivers down her spine. As she looked up at her, Gypsy realized she had no choice but to do her bidding. Not because of guilt or Cleos's command to protect her. She needed to do it because killing the child was the only way to ensure the safety of everyone, and she needed to see it through to the end—to make sure it was done, and done right.

31

M URDER IS NOT SUPPOSED to be simple or easy, and yet it is. Gypsy and Cori had argued for some time about the path by which the child would leave this world. Despite Gypsy's insistence on using a sedative or an injection to stop the heart, Cori was determined to have his heart stopped by a singular puncture wound. That was why she wanted Gypsy to do it. Her background in medicine, both educational and experiential, would ensure a direct hit.

Gypsy stared at the metal pick with a fancy embellished medallion perched at the top. It was no more a weapon than any other household device, but it would do the job. Especially if she pierced the heart as Cori demanded. Yet, it still seemed an odd choice. Almost as if this were a sacrificial ceremony instead of an execution. Gypsy's mind flooded with images of that boy strapped down to an altar again. There was something truly disturbing about it to her. She felt as if someone had strapped her to it, and yet, now especially, she also felt like the man wielding the knife to kill the boy.

Gypsy stared down at Cori's son, properly splayed for his sacrifice—stilled by the power of her unintentional spell. She felt a coldness wrap around her heart—something heinous and evil was pushing its way into her, but since she was already immune to the battles of light and dark, it just felt like a gnawing sensation in her brain. A reminder that bad things happen all the time and there was no sense in drowning along with all the others.

That wasn't the way heroes were supposed to behave. They were supposed to empathize with victims and torment themselves with the havoc they reap—even on their enemies. But as Cori reminded her, she was no hero. She was the next best thing to Daniel McGrath—a beautiful monster with a purpose.

Just as Leona had to live up to the burdens of her werewolf heritage, Gypsy had to use her own psychoses for the betterment of others. She had to sacrifice the last tiny shred of humanity she had left and break her most sacred rule.

She had to kill a child.

It would be her prevailing good deed and her most damning act all in one. When the time came, she could use it as a credit to pay the ferryman for her trip into hell.

At that moment, Gypsy despised how well she understood human anatomy. How she instinctively knew where to place the tip and at what angle to maximize the damage and minimize the pain. It would be quick either way—a bee sting at best, followed by a forever sleep. Humane... at least for the child.

Gypsy took a breath and pushed. Another flash of memory briefly blinded her—sun, chains, blood, screams. Then there was an audible pop—like a needle pushing through thick denim. After that, the long spike slid into the boy's chest with no further tension. Gypsy couldn't help but think that it felt wrong. The heart should be tougher than that—it should offer some resistance, but then again, she had never stabbed the heart of a child.

More visions of the genie's memories swirled around her. She tried to push away the thoughts, but they demanded to be seen, heard, and felt. The angry buzzing bees attacked her mind, showing her images of a dying boy strapped to an altar. She was floating above him. He was screaming and crying, covered in blood. The surge of power that entered him without his consent would forever change his world.

His back arched, and he took in an almost endless inhalation. Once he had drawn in the last of the air, he stopped moving. He froze, staring up at her, eyes wide and glistening with the last of his tears. A single bead of moisture fell from his eye and landed on the altar. It mixed with the blood dripping from the boy's back.

It wasn't until then that Gypsy could see the source of the blood. A knife was embedded in his chest. The sacred blade was meant to give the boy death and life with the same strike. Much as Gypsy had observed the battle between Danato and Ethan earlier, she looked at this boy with the same reverence.

Sadness and anger were easy to see when he was in motion. The pain of death was written in the blood all around him, but that wasn't what held her captive. Beyond the blood and the tears, Gypsy could see something inside the boy. Or perhaps she felt it. Something was shifting in him—transforming him from something ordinary to something beyond words—and it was beautiful.

This wasn't death as she had witnessed so many times before. However, it wasn't the life his murderers suggested it would be either. There was no more fear. There was no more want. There was nothing—and yet, there was everything.

Time, space, light, sound, energy, and matter.

For a moment, just a moment longer than all the rest of her hallucination—Gypsy could see the stars. Not some. Not many, but all of them. A cascade of lights shone brightly and dimmed away, as time—past, present, and future—became an irrational concept to her. The universe unfolded before her, offering all its glory as a singular gift. A burdensome gift—no less arduous than it was magnificent, but only a fool would say no. And that boy, from so many, many years ago, was not a fool.

The power merged with him, and his body—unable to hold such energy as a physical being—melted away, turning from flesh to smoke. The knife that had punctured his heart became an oil lamp. The smoke swirled into thin rivulets and slithered into its new home. The spell that had created the genie marked his skin with tattoos and placed carvings on the lamp—proof of a time when men were powerful enough to make their own gods.

Gypsy's vision ceased, and her capacity to see beyond her human comprehension failed, leaving her bereft. She stared down at the boy in her arms. His body was limp, head sagging against her forearm. His skin had gone instantly cold and looked sallow. His bright little eyes rolled back slightly. Gypsy quickly brushed her fingers down his face to close them so she didn't have to look at them any longer. She wanted so much for him to turn into smoke and float away—live semi-happily ever after in a lamp to grant wishes as he saw fit, but he didn't. He was no longer a vessel the genie could use.

Gypsy's stomach lurched as she looked up at the clock. The second hand was ticking away as normal. The spell must have broken just as she brought down her scythe.

It was over.

A choice had been made.

And justly so, right or wrong, the woman who had brought him into this world made that choice.

Cori reached past her, pressing her fingers to the flat disk that topped the pick. For a moment, Gypsy thought she intended to pull it back out, which for some reason made her gag. "No, don't—"

With a deft twist, the top of the murder weapon snapped off in Cori's grip, leaving the metal tip still in the boy's heart. Gypsy watched her stuff the broken piece into her back pocket. She then wrapped an emergency fire blanket around her son and pulled him from Gypsy's arms. She tugged the blanket up around his shoulders and over his head—covering his face and the small dot of blood on his tiny shirt that read, "Mama's boy."

Gypsy shifted to look at her, trying to see what state of grief she was in. Since she wasn't screaming and pounding the floor in futility, Gypsy thought perhaps she was in the silent sobbing stage, but there were no tears. Gypsy, of all people, had no right to judge how a woman handled her emotions, but she knew Cori well enough to expect some reaction.

"Cori," Gypsy whispered and reached out to touch her. A gesture of reassurance, more acted upon than heartfelt, but nonetheless important at this moment. The second her fingers brushed against Cori's hand, a wave of emotion hit her. The intensity of which was as strong as when she touched the blood of Adrianna.

She repelled herself from Cori, gasping and panting as she tried to shake off whatever she felt. Was all of that inside of Cori?

Impossible.

It was too much.

Gypsy stared at Cori wide-eyed, and she stared right back at her. Concern flitted over her features as she tried to figure out what was wrong with her. "What's wrong?" Cori took a step toward her.

"No!" Gypsy raised her hands in surrender. Never in her life had she surrendered—certainly not without a gun in her face. But right now, Cori frightened her down to the deepest part of her soul. She couldn't take any further disruption to her balance. God only knows what would happen if she lost control. If she finally broke. Whose blood would spill then? Cori had told her she was just one bad day from becoming the woman from her altered reality. Was this that bad day? Had breaking her only rule thrown her so far off the rails that she was about to crash?

As strange as she was behaving already, Gypsy felt tears streaming down her cheeks. Why was she crying? Cori should be the one crying.

That bothered Gypsy. A mother must grieve. It's not natural. It's not right.

Cori seemed to realize she was not helping Gypsy's tenuous hold on her sanity. She frowned and backed away from her. She pulled her son close to her and headed to the open elevator awaiting her arrival.

When the doors closed and Gypsy thought the carriage had moved down far enough to give her privacy, she clenched her fists tight, opened her mouth wide, and let out a feral scream.

<h1 style="text-align:center">32</h1>

DANATO NEVER COULD HAVE imagined a scenario in which his loyal successor would defy him... until now. He couldn't blame Ethan for defending his flesh and blood. Had he not been hardened by loss and conscripted to his duty by his lineage, he too might be fighting for the life of his grandson instead of fighting to kill him.

Danato raised Ethan off the floor, trying to contain his reaction so they didn't have to resort to a hand-to-hand fight. However, Ethan was not as easily subdued as he had hoped. He used Danato's arms for leverage to climb his body and kick him in the face. He dropped Ethan and stumbled back, clutching his aching cheek. "Stop this!" he demanded as Ethan ran forward to hit him again.

Danato had never been quick. The dragon serum usually acted to intensify a man's existing talents. That meant that Ethan was strong and agile. He was a natural fighter and, given the right circumstances, he could well bring down a man twice his size.

Danato, on the other hand had been born strong. He was a big baby, a bulky teenager, and with the help of magic—he was even stronger than he looked. A skill that no one, not even Belus, knew the full extent of. It was not something he wanted anyone to know. It was not something that anyone should ever need to know.

Despite his demands, Ethan didn't relent. He was playing his part as the hero of this story. Danato understood that—he loved him for it. He only wished that he didn't have to be the villain once again. He had never wanted to be an executioner. The one who balances lives against the rules of his job.

But this decision wasn't about his title anymore. It was about humanity and the Earth. The power of the universe could not rest on the shoulders of a child. It was too much to hold, let alone wield. Even if the boy survived the induction of power that was about to be foisted upon him—which was impossible—then he would be just as insane as the wizards. The potential for chaos at the hands of a temperamental toddler with the cosmos at his fingertips was only one scenario. The earth—disrupted by the imbalance of power—could spur a catastrophic chain reaction of natural disasters that would ultimately kill humanity. And even then, if that was not what happened, there was still the potential for a paradoxical rippling. A concept that was still only theoretical, but involved all matter connected to earth magic mirroring its position with cosmic matter—effectively the destruction of time and space itself.

Everywhere Danato looked, there were more reasons not to allow the genie to access the boy. As much as he loved him, and as sure as he was that killing him would sever his relationship with Ethan and Cori completely, he knew he had to do what was right. He had to save the world and spare his grandchild the pain of being its destroyer.

Ethan's fist hit him in the chin before he could stop it. From any other man, it may not have even hurt, but Danato felt it like a brick against his jaw. Then another brick hit his cheek. Then his temple.

Another and another.

Danato stumbled back, protected only by his resistance to being knocked out. He realized at that moment that Ethan was no longer himself. He was a raging beast not unlike the man Danato became after he gave the order to have his wife killed. Ethan was not defending his son; he was already avenging him. There was only one way to put a stop to this fight now, and it didn't appeal to him any more than the duties of the rest of his day.

Blood dripped into Danato's eyes from cuts on his brows, making it impossible to see Ethan's swift attacks well enough to block them. He reached out blindly and found a neck in front of him. He grabbed on tight—but not tight enough to snap it.

He pushed forward with a roar that matched the brute he appeared to be. Lifting slightly, he brought Ethan up in the air before throwing him down. He knew he was about to break his back. Ethan would recover, of course, but still... It was more violence than he had ever used against an underling before, and he didn't like to do it.

Instead of the slap of a body landing hard against the floor, Danato heard the crunch of something and an effeminate moan. Confused by the sounds, he wiped his eyes to get a better look at what he had accomplished. Instead of Ethan, he held Leona in his grip. The white tiles she was lying on had cracked, and dust from the concrete under them was sifting out. She looked up at him, a little annoyed, but mostly she was just in pain.

He frowned and swung around to see where Ethan had ended up. He was across the room, on the floor, panting and leering at Danato. Levi was at his side, his hands clamped tightly to his shoulders—not entirely holding him down, but judging by the way Ethan kept trying to lunge forward, the young man must have been doing something to hold him back.

Danato turned to Efrat, who was protecting the child. The elemental shook his head slowly, a definite determination in his eyes. Once again, Danato found room to respect Efrat for his loyal obstinacy, but now was not the time to test Danato's compassion. "Move!" he demanded.

"Don't you touch him!" Ethan yelled and burst from Levi's grip.

Danato didn't give Efrat a second chance. He punched the elemental in the chest. An audible crack confirmed he had broken a rib or two. Efrat winced and lost focus on his power. He dropped to the floor, and the veil of blue came down within.

Ethan arrived to continue the fight, but Danato didn't give him the opportunity for another target. He dodged Ethan's punch, grabbed his wrist, and launched his body across the room. He hit the wall, damaging the sheetrock before dropping to the ground.

He caught Belus's eye before he turned around and noted that there was no surprise on his face. He gave him a nod as if giving him permission to do what must be done. It wasn't much, but it was the support he needed to complete his horrific duty.

He turned back to pick up the boy, but he wasn't there. His eyes fluttered around the area, searching for where the child could hide from him. He hated the idea of hunting him down, but there wasn't much time left. Soon the genie would claim him, and a power beyond human comprehension would rest in the hands of a child.

"He's gone," Leona croaked.

Danato looked back at her. Judging by how little she had moved, he must have caused her a great deal of pain. If she hadn't been a werewolf, he might have killed her. As it was, though, he was wondering why she had put herself in his path. She had no doubt pushed Ethan out of the way, and his blindness left him to grab the first neck within reach.

Why, though? Why was she involved in this mess? Since when had she become the protective type?

"What do you mean, *gone*?" He stepped closer to her. To his surprise, she flinched slightly when his boots got close to her. As if she expected him to kick her while she was down. Despite this obvious concern, she did not attempt to get away from him.

She chuckled slightly. "You didn't really think that she would let you kill her child, did you? You should know more than anyone that she's a pain in the ass."

"Leona, what has she done?" Danato felt panic sweep over him—his skin prickled as a cold sweat covered his entire body. He needed to stop the genie. He needed to find the boy. "Where is he?"

Leona laughed again, and Danato raised his foot over her—threatening to press it against her already tender body. She instantly stopped laughing and stared at his foot like a venomous snake. "Don't make me hurt you, Leona. I need to stop this. You *know* I do. All of you know that I have to do this!" Danato included Efrat and Ethan in his conclusion.

"No, you don't," Cori said from the doorway of the section break. Unlike Danato, she sounded perfectly calm.

"Cori! Get out of here!" Leona screamed at her.

Danato stared at Cori. Her son was wrapped up in a blanket, slumped against her shoulder. His heart had no room left to hurt, but he could still muster his anger when he looked at her. "I'm sorry, sweetheart, you know I don't want to do this. If there were any other way, I would have taken it."

"I know," Cori answered numbly.

"Please." He eased his way around Leona. "Give the boy to me."

"Cori, don't let him touch him!" Ethan yelled, struggling to get himself off the floor. Danato may not have broken his back, but he had hurt him. "Just run! Get out of here!"

Cori looked at him somberly and shook her head. "It's too late for that." Even as the words left her mouth, a swirling column of smoke appeared between Danato and her.

"Cori, give him to me!" Danato moved forward, reaching out for the child. He knew he could make it quick and painless for the boy. He just needed to get to him before it was too late.

Electricity hit Danato in the back. He gritted his teeth against the pain, but despite his sheer will, he couldn't fight against Efrat's oppressive power. He dropped to his knees with a groan. He looked up at Cori, pleading with his eyes for her to bring the child to him. He hated to ask this of her, but it was now or never.

Cori stared down at him, sympathetic to his pain, but by no means interested in helping him or doing his bidding.

As the smoke settled, the genie took form. First the legs, then the muscular torso, and finally his bald head. As the genie solidified, Efrat's attack diminished into static and then eventually nothing—as if the cosmic force within the room had sapped out every last drop of earth magic—including the elemental branch. Yet another reminder to Danato that fighting this creation was not an option.

The genie's eyes opened—sparkling and exuding life in a way that no human eyes could. He turned his head to acknowledge everyone in the room. His gaze settled on Levi. He frowned and shook his head. "You don't belong here."

"Neither do you," Levi said like a sullen child. He even crossed his arms as if to pout about the accusation. Danato looked between the two of them, not liking anything resembling familiarity between the two men.

The genie let out a deep, cavernous laugh and nodded. "How right you are, little one." He turned his attention to Cori next and smiled at her. "Hello, Corinthia."

Her numb expression turned into subdued adulation. It was something everyone felt in the presence of his power. Danato was much better at hiding it than most, but Cori seemed particularly drawn to this being. He thought perhaps it had to do with her previous interactions with him—or possibly she was just vulnerable because of her many experiences involving psychic violations. "Hello," she said softly and took a step toward him.

"Cori," Belus admonished her. Her head turned slightly, acknowledging his words, but then she continued forward. "Cori!" Belus snapped, but she stopped on her own, mere inches from the demi-god.

The genie seemed to enjoy this and shifted his body to face her. "Don't touch," he warned, though there was a genuine look of intrigue in his eyes as if he really wanted her to touch him. Danato pulled himself off the floor and moved to yank Cori away before the genie's celestial allure drew her in.

"It's over," Cori said flatly. Danato stopped behind her, hand still outstretched to pull her back.

The genie tilted his head curiously at her. "Over?"

"The child is out of your grasp," she clarified. "You'll never have him."

Danato looked at the motionless bundle resting against Cori's shoulder. He could just see the top of her son's head through a gap in the blanket. His breath caught in his throat as he caught sight of the pale white skin of his forehead. Much too pale.

Danato tried to piece together the last twenty minutes—the merman, the near misses, the child appearing and disappearing before their very eyes. He didn't fully understand the how, but the why was becoming clearer. The only thing he knew for certain was that the decision he had committed himself to—the choice only a warden should have to make—had already been made. The hand of the executioner had not been stayed. It had only been passed on. Passed on to his successor.

Danato's hand slowly descended, no longer reaching toward anything. He stepped away from Cori and the genie. His footing felt weak, and his breathing came in stutters instead of solid breaths. He turned to Belus to see if he was seeing what he had. His second was already looking at the bundle in Cori's arms warily. It took only the expression on Danato's face to confirm what he suspected. Belus's eyes lowered to the floor—and he didn't look back up.

It was what they both intended. It was the right answer—the only answer. And yet... it still hurt.

"What's going on?" Ethan asked. He hadn't moved far from the wall—only enough to see the interaction between Cori and the genie. He was looking at everyone, searching for an answer. He knew something was wrong, but he couldn't see it.

Cori looked at Ethan, and for a long moment, she just stared at him. The gaze fixed on him was one of dread, but she eventually found her voice again. "It's over, Ethan." She shifted away from the genie and bent down low. She shifted her child's body off her shoulder and placed him gently onto the glossy white floor. The blanket covering him flopped back, revealing the boy's sallow features to everyone.

Leona gasped and reached out for the toddler, despite being too far to reach him. "No," she whimpered as if it were her own child lying there dead.

"What?" Ethan danced around, not quite approaching his son. "No," he whispered, still searching Cori for a truth that didn't align with what his eyes were seeing. He huffed several times as he paced closer to the body with every pass. "No," he repeated.

Efrat scoffed loudly and started laughing, though there was nothing cheerful in the noise. "This fuckin' place," he murmured. Danato caught his eye, and Efrat directed all of his anger and disappointment at him. Not so much the bitter disloyalty that he usually expressed, but something new. Something that said he was finally seeing Danato for who he was, and he was even more displeased with this villain than the one he had created in his mind. "This fucking place eats you alive! Do you know that? Do you get that?" he asked.

"Yes," Danato answered pitilessly before looking back at the genie. "The contract is broken. The child is no longer *of warm blood*. Leave genie," he commanded, though he had little recourse if the being didn't do as he bid.

The genie looked at him but aimed his response at Cori. "You're a foolish woman with no understanding of the power I possess. Defying me does not serve your best interests."

Cori stood from her son and faced the genie. "I am not defying you, genie. I'm denying you. These are your rules. I'm just playing the game differently than you expected."

"This is not a win for anyone." The genie glanced at Ethan, who was shaking. Tears were pouring from his eyes, though no tormented sobs were audible. The genie narrowed his eyes at Cori and shook his head—a gentle castigation. "I have no wish to fight with you."

Cori's brow perked. "If you don't want to fight me, then leave and never return."

"Oh, if only it were that simple."

"You heard her!" Gypsy's voice carried over from the entrance as she stumbled inside. She looked disheveled and sweaty. She had dark circles under her bloodshot eyes. Danato wasn't sure if she was wounded or drunk. "She said get the fuck out of here." The genie looked Gypsy over before determining that he was not concerned with her. He reached down as if to pick up the child, but Gypsy screamed at him, "Hey!" The genie looked back at her—baffled. "I said... get... your... cosmic... motherfuckin' ass... out of here."

"Do you really want to play this game with me again, mortal?"

Gypsy cracked a smile, revealing bloody teeth as she let out a breathy cackle. Before she could contribute her usual signature smack talk, her head tipped to one side, and she groaned. She pressed a finger into her ear and wiggled it. "Shhh!" She ripped her finger out of her ear and waved it at no one in particular. "Shh. Shh. Shh." Her insistence seemed to silence whatever she had been hearing.

The genie shifted closer to examine her. "What are you?" he asked with a tone that revealed his disdain for her.

Gypsy looked up, eyes glittering with something resembling her former self. She raised her hands and shoved his chest. Danato tensed, waiting for the excruciating torment that would follow contact with a genie, but it never came. The genie stumbled back, visibly shocked by her ability to touch him without consequence. To add insult to injury, she did it again, nearly toppling him this time.

"What are you!" he yelled at her, his voice no longer soothing and Zen, but rather the roar of the cosmos demanding answers from a pathetic mortal.

"I am the altar! I am the chains! I am the boy! I am the blade! I am the blood!" Gypsy ranted—spitting her words at the genie. "Shhh!" She hissed, waving her hands at her imaginary disruptions. For a moment, she was herself again—dead eyes locked onto her target and ready for battle. "I am the one telling you to get the fuck out of here!" She raised her hands again and pushed him again. The genie winced and recoiled away from her hands. Danato thought he could see the tattoos on his skin move—as if they too were recoiling from Gypsy's touch.

"I would listen to her," Levi said. His voice was a surprise, as it usually was, but Danato hadn't noticed that he had come to Leona's aid. He was holding her hand, stroking it gently. Once again, thoughts of when this relationship had developed popped into his mind, but he didn't have time to get those answers.

The genie looked at Levi, but he still seemed reluctant to acknowledge any weakness. Gypsy took advantage of his distraction and came at him for the third time. She gritted her teeth and roared as if she were putting every last angry thought into her punch. When her fist impacted the genie, he instantly turned to smoke.

It swirled and danced around Gypsy for a moment. She bit at it like a dog trying to catch a nuisance fly. It eventually dissipated into nothing, and Gypsy dropped to the floor. She laughed maniacally at the ceiling . Levi launched to her side, and she grabbed onto him, pulling on his shirt to bring him down to her. "What's happening to me?" she asked him.

"I'm not sure, but I think I can help."

"She did this to me, didn't she?" she asked.

Levi glanced at Danato before answering. "Maybe."

"Why? Why would she give this to me?"

"I don't know."

Danato narrowed his eyes at this interaction, and he opened his mouth to demand answers for Gypsy's sudden resistance to the genie, but Ethan interrupted him.

"What happened!" Ethan yelled, still trying to get a grasp on the situation. He looked at Danato and Cori before collapsing next to his son. He picked him up and pressed him to his ear. He was trying to hear his heartbeat, but it didn't take a doctor to confirm that the child was dead. When, who, and how were the only questions left to answer, but Danato already knew the answer to one of those questions, and that was enough truth to tide him over for now.

Cori's eyes were now pleading with him for immunity against his rage. Danato couldn't deny her that. And of course he had to forgive her. Forgive her for the action he was about to undertake himself. However, against his will, his eyes drifted down, not willing or able to hold her gaze.

"What happened!" Ethan roared. "Who did this?" he finally voiced the question that his mind was not allowing him to believe without proof.

The room went silent—even the riled mermaids were keeping still. Danato looked at Cori. He knew the answer—probably everyone did, but she still had to say it.

"I did," Cori said the words and Ethan's face fell. His shoulders sagged, and he placed his son back on the floor carefully, as if he might still be able to damage him. He stood slowly and stared at her.

"You did this?" he asked in barely a whisper. "You killed our son?"

"I had to, Ethan. It was the only way to protect everyone."

His eyes danced over her, searching for something. Perhaps he just thought he didn't recognize her.

"I can explain."

His eyes glazed, and his grief evaporated into something dark. Something Danato had never seen in him before. Certainly not while he was looking at Cori.

Danato was looking right at him, but he still didn't see the movement. Two steps or three, it didn't matter—one second Ethan was standing there and the next he was on top of Cori. He had pinned her to the ground and wrapped his hands around her throat.

Danato jumped forward and grabbed for him, but he couldn't get Ethan's hands off her throat. His grip just slipped away, unable to get purchase. He was reliving a moment from the past—a déjà vu that made him sick to his stomach. "Belus!" he yelled, and his second arrived a moment later.

Between Danato trying to pull on his arms and Belus prying at his fingers, they should have been able to remove him. Ethan wasn't this strong. Surely not stronger than both of them.

Levi jumped in with them, trying to use his natural anti-magic to calm Ethan, but nothing he said or did was taking vengeance from the man's eyes. Ethan intended to murder Cori, and there was nothing anyone could do to stop him.

Cori struggled and fought, hitting him and kicking him anywhere she could, but she couldn't do anything more than Danato and Belus. Her eyes were bulging and tearing up. Instead, she moved one grappling hand to Danato's and squeezed his fingers tight. She must have realized she was about to die. Her other hand frantically moved up and down trying to reach around the mess of hands that were killing and trying to save her. She moved her hand from his and grabbed his shirt. She yanked on the front pocket forcefully, nearly ripping it off. Her face went from red to blue, and her eyes glazed over.

"Move!" Efrat yelled over Danato's frantic plea for Ethan to stop. Static electricity filled the air. Belus looked up and scrambled away from Cori. Danato did the same, dragging Levi back with him.

Danato only caught a glimpse of the energy dancing off Efrat's hands before thunder nearly deafened him and a bright light forced him to shield his eyes. The next thing he heard beyond a steady ringing was coughing and heavy breathing.

He rolled over and crawled to Cori. She was struggling to get out from under Ethan's unconscious body. He pulled her free and pressed her against his chest. Following her bouts of coughing, she began to cry, and he did the same.

Everything was ruined.

The happy little family he had harvested from rocky soil had just imploded. Nothing was ever going to be the same again.

And beyond that terrible realization, he had questions. So many questions.

He watched Efrat pacing quietly at the edge of the room. He seemed to want to come over to Cori, but wouldn't as long as she was in Danato's arms. Perhaps for that reason alone, he held her a little tighter.

Levi was back to tending to Gypsy, who was now endeavoring to kick Ethan while he was unconscious. Levi pulled her back, assuring her that Ethan was already out cold. He spoke to her gently as if she were now a child and not the sociopathic bitch that everyone knew and hated. What had changed in her? Why was she defending Cori instead of taunting her? And more importantly, how the hell had she been able to bully a demi-god?

Belus was on the floor leaning against the wall—staring out at nothing. This was the second time he and Belus would endure the chosen death of a close loved one. They would each do their best to hide behind their hard edges, but with Cori being the trigger this time, he wasn't sure they would fare so well. They couldn't blame each other for this loss, and they surely couldn't focus their anger on Cori—not when she had just made the greatest sacrifice of all. This time, they might just have to face their grief.

Leona was still on the floor where he had left her, confirming that he had indeed broken her back. A crime for which he would no doubt still have to pay for. He would have thought hurting Leona was impossible, but then again, he had never tussled with a fem-wolf before. Could he really be strong enough to break her bones?

And of course, in the center of it all was his grandchild. Dead. Murdered by his own mother for the sake of the entire human race. It didn't matter what gallant phrase he put behind it or how many rationalizations he paired with it. A child had still been killed. And for the third time in such a brief span, they would mourn the loss of one of their own.

33

Leona gasped when Danato touched her hand. He had assumed that she was asleep, but apparently, she was only resting. He raised his hand in surrender and gently shushed her. "Easy," he said and sat down in the metal chair next to her bed. She eyed him carefully as he did. "How are you feeling?"

She stared at him, anger rising in her eyes. "Fine," she snapped as if his question was a hit against her pride.

"Leona, you must know. I didn't realize who I was grabbing when I—"

"I had to intervene. You might have killed Ethan."

Danato shook his head. He wasn't that far out of control.

"At the very least, he would be in this bed instead of me."

"About that," Danato broached the topic as carefully as he could.

"You must be pleased to have injured a fem-wolf? That's a feat not often achieved by men—human men."

Danato's lip twitched. "Why would that please me?"

"Oh, come now, Danato, you must find some delight in having me in such a debilitated state."

Danato sighed, disappointed that the woman he had shared coffee with earlier that day was just in a passing mood. "Leona, the doctor took several X-rays of your spine. He found some anomalies beyond your injury, so I gave him permission to do further scans."

Leona scoffed. "That wasn't necessary. I'll heal in no time—regardless of what you have done to me."

Danato wasn't used to having this type of conversation. If he hadn't caused her injury to begin with, he might have let the doctor be the one to speak with her. Unfortunately, the doctor was also very much afraid of her and didn't want to give her his diagnosis. "They found micro-fractures in your bones."

Leona smiled at him. "I'm a werewolf, Danato. We get micro-fractures all the time."

"Yes, but you have an inordinate number of them. Tell me about the hormone replacement you have been using. Are there any side effects?"

Leona sighed and shrugged. "It's still new, but there are issues with muscle loss and bone density, but that is to be expected. The change itself rebuilds us from the ground up. Without that, we are bound to get a little weaker."

Danato nodded. "Yes, I imagine so. The doctor and I discussed your case at length, but of course, without the data from your doctors, he only has conjecture to base his diagnosis on."

"Diagnosis?" Leona laughed. "Don't sound so serious."

"Leona, may I ask how many transformations you have missed since you discovered this hormonal therapy?"

Leona looked at the ceiling and counted in her head. "I suppose technically six."

"Technically?"

"The first two doses still allowed for partial transformations, so I can't claim them as a successful procedure."

Danato nodded and looked down at his hands.

"Why are you being so serious?"

He looked up at her and smiled. "You know, of all the creatures I have encountered, I still find werewolves to be the most fascinating species."

Leona smiled back at him, unable to hide her appreciation for his flattery. "Go on."

"The metamorphosis you go through in such a short time is phenomenal. I truly believe that if it weren't for your shortened life spans, you would be the dominating species on the earth and, sadly, humans would be your pets."

Leona laughed. "I wish I could tell you I haven't had this conversation already, but my kin are very egotistical—as you know."

"I do know." Danato chuckled, thinking of Vince. He was a good friend, but he was a bit of an ass. He was never one to hide his place on the food chain. However, he would gladly take another hit to his ego to see him again. To playfully banter with his friend. "It's in that miraculous metamorphosis that you find yourself with that shortened lifespan, so I understand your desire to avoid it. And it makes sense... at least on the surface."

Leona frowned. "What are you trying to tell me, Danato?"

"I'm sure you know the sordid details of your own change, but I'm not sure that werewolves are frequently taught the science of it. I mean the down-and-dirty cellular analysis."

"We try to focus on the ceremony of it. Two minds confined to one body. Not many want the down-and-dirty version."

"I'm not a scientist, but as I said, I've always been fascinated by the change, so I'm going to try to sum up a few of the key characteristics." Leona narrowed her eyes but bobbed her head in approval. She could no doubt sense Danato's urgency to speak, but also his reluctance. It made for a confusing set of emotions—even for him. "Skipping the muscle expansion and skin stretching and the hair growth—none of it would be possible without the elasticity of your bones. This is where the similarities to humans end, and you become something altogether foreign. A perfect balance between flexibility and strength, a werewolf's bones are designed to soften and elongate. After which, they solidify again. Giving them the strength to hold the inflated muscles of the wolf form."

"Yes, allowing us to be stronger than any animal on earth."

Danato nodded. "Doubtlessly." He paused before ruining the compliment. "But that form cannot be maintained."

"Of course not; it's always been temporary."

"No, I mean—physically—if it were possible to remain a wolf, you would die within a very short time. The stress of that form is too great. Even if the heart didn't give out, the body itself would start to break down—muscle failure, bone breaks, and..." Danato trailed off. Leona was not enjoying his tale of weakness about her celebrated form. She wasn't quite glaring at him, so much as staring through him. He cleared his throat and stood to get some distance between them.

He checked the nurse's station through the window, where several women were still dabbing their eyes. Danato was ignorant to think that the boy's death would affect only a few of them. Cori's son had been a ray of sunshine in this drab, inhospitable world. The nursing staff had doted on him and spoiled him every chance they got. They would fight for the duty to babysit when Ethan and Cori had conflicting schedules. News had traveled fast about Cori's... choice. No one knew what to make of it. They would have had no trouble accepting *his* moral failure. He would have spent the better part of the year receiving unfriendly glares, cold shoulders, and even colder coffee.

And he gladly would have embraced that punishment and so much more.

But Cori... His own mother...

They were all trying to swallow the lumps in their throats and attempting to make sense of why she had volunteered herself for such an unpleasant act. Why hadn't she let him spare her that memory? Why hadn't she just let him be the bad guy?

It didn't matter now. It was done. The genie had irreparably changed their world. The only thing he could do was put himself back to work, because regardless of how much it hurt to do so—he still had a prison to run.

"The fact is," Danato continued as he paced the room, ignoring the weeping nurses. "The bones endure more than minor fractures while in the wolf state. It's believed the micro-fractures that most werewolves possess are due to bone breakage during their wolf state. But once you transform back, the sheer volume of osteoclasts and osteoblasts basically rebuilds the bone. In young werewolves, the restructuring can actually make the bones stronger and therefore allow for even better muscle development."

"I am being terribly patient with you, Danato, but if you have a point to make, you really should make it."

"Our doctor is concerned about the long-term ramifications of missing your lunar phase." Leona scoffed, obviously not impressed by the opinion of a human doctor. "I know this is an important step in normalizing your life and potentially bringing werewolves back into the public fold, but I'm concerned that the methods being used are rushed and not yet safe."

"Don't be ridiculous."

"You're lying in a hospital bed with a broken back." Danato motioned to her immobile state.

"You are an abnormally strong man."

"Yes, I am, but I am still a man. I was able to shatter three of your vertebrae because your body is littered with potential breaking points. The daily pressure of your human form is also a significant stress to your bones. Without the change, you can't repair these micro-fractures. Without the change, you cannot maintain your bone strength. It is our diagnosis that if you continue with these procedures, you will start to lose bone density and potentially become permanently crippled. What's worse is there is a strong likelihood that there will be a point of no return—in which a transformation would kill you instead of heal you."

"Then my doctors will need to find a solution."

"They probably already have; they just haven't told you about it."

"What are you talking about?"

"Catabolic hormones."

Leona frowned, but Danato waited for her to ask. "What is that?"

"They will reduce your muscle mass—make you weaker." Leona's eyes lit with anger, and her mouth struggled to form the words of castigation, which she no doubt wanted to throw at him. Danato moved back to her bed and sat down again. "Don't you see what you are doing, Leona? By removing the change, you are just sacrificing the very thing that makes you superior. Once the wolf is gone, its strength goes with it. You will be effectively... a human."

Leona's face contorted with grief—no doubt disgusted with the thought of being average. Her ego wouldn't allow that. Danato thought she might cry, but she just held a mortified expression and stared at her legs. "What if I want that?" she whispered.

"What?"

She turned to him and let the words once again meekly slip from her lips. "What if I want to be... human?"

Danato shook his head vigorously. He didn't believe these words. He couldn't believe these words. "Leona, you aren't yourself right now—"

"Would you think less of me?"

Danato's mouth gaped, but he couldn't really think of how he thought of her before this moment, let alone now.

"I'm not allowed to want less for myself. That's against the rules—isn't it? I thought I could have it both ways, but I should have listened to old lore. I didn't need science to tell me this. The stories of werewolf heritage always said that the wolf is what gives us our strength. If we lose the wolf, so goes our strength." Leona shook her head.

"When you're feeling better, I want you to speak to our doctor. I want you to consider all of your options. Losing the wolf doesn't have to be an all-or-nothing decision. There may be a way to lessen the number of transformations—or the degree—while still achieving the structural repairs." Danato reached out again and touched her hand. She looked down at the contact. "I think it would be unwise to make a decision about your future until you understand how these hormones might be affecting your... temperament."

Leona stared at him. "Do you think if the child had lived he would be two beings like me?"

"What do you mean?"

"Do you think part of him would have been human and the other part god? Constantly fighting with himself to be one or the other?"

Danato took a breath and shook his head. "No, Leona. I think if the child had lived, he would have ceased to exist. And we would all be suffering for it."

"She did the right thing then?"

Danato stood and pawed at his shirt, adjusting it unnecessarily. "Right or wrong, it was the only choice."

"Then why do you hate her for it?"

Danato shook his head, dismissing her interpretation of his emotions. "I could never hate Cori, but I do hate what I've turned her into." He stared down at the floor for a moment. "It just never occurred to me that..."

"That she was capable of murder?" Leona asked.

Danato shook his head. He wasn't sure what he wanted to say. Cori had always been a fighter, and murder may not have been her target, but she didn't have the luxury of nonlethal defense. It had never been a question of Cori's ability to kill, but rather what could provoke her to act on that instinct.

Ethan, on the other hand, was strong enough to defend himself and others without lethal intent. He had never been faced with the no-win scenarios that Cori had. And as a result, there was no blood on his conscience.

Since executing Adrianna, Danato's relationship with Ethan had become tense. His obligation to restrict magical superiority was putting a wedge between them. He would never have predicted that such a basic rule could make Ethan's loyalty waver. He wondered if his successor would ever have the stomach to be the warden this prison needed. Now, more than ever, it seemed Cori was the one with the gumption. She had committed to her duty and put the safety of the world ahead of her son. Danato should have been proud of her, but the emotion he really felt was disappointment.

34

Pain had been redefined.

Ethan thought nothing could hurt as much as losing his best friends. He even imagined that losing his child in some accidental way would be far preferable to this agony. To know that Cori caused and implemented his pain herself made him livid. It was the same anger that spurred him into a blackout rage that almost killed her. One that he still hadn't quite recovered from. One that, if given the opportunity, he might repeat.

He had to get away from her, away from this place—away from everything.

Ethan stared down at the crate that was marked "animal food." There had to be some great joke about Daniel McGrath's final resting place being labeled "animal food," but he couldn't think of one. It was the kind of joke Daniel himself would have been ready and waiting in the wings with.

The doc manager had questioned Ethan about the legitimacy of his hand-delivering Daniel's remains. It was not normal protocol, but by rights, bypassing the crematorium was already against protocol. The fact that he didn't have permission to leave was the real issue. However, Ethan was determined to get the hell out of this place. Returning Daniel's body to his mother was just an excuse.

It took only one glare from Ethan to get the manager on board for the transfer. News traveled fast in the prison, and even though it had only been a matter of hours since his son had turned up in the prison morgue—he knew that everyone already knew his life had been turned upside down. He was no longer the man they knew. He was just flesh and bone over a ravaged soul.

"Heading out?" Efrat asked from the entryway.

Ethan turned his head slowly and looked at him leaning against the doorframe. The man was never relaxed, but he tried to portray it. A smart tactic in case Ethan might see him as a threat. He was well aware the burn mark on his back was from Efrat. It caused him excruciating pain with even the slightest movement, but he was glad of it. He was glad there was a constant punishment to remind him of what he had almost done.

Ethan was grateful Efrat had fought by his side to help save his son. When the argument finally came to blows, it wasn't Danato on his side. It was Efrat. He stood at his side ready to defend his son to the death. Had it been Duke there, Ethan wasn't sure if he could have expected that much loyalty from him. And had it been Daniel...

There wouldn't have been an argument to begin with if Daniel had been there.

Ethan pulled his long wool trench coat tight and buttoned it up as he moved to the edge of the dock to look down at the elemental. "Daniel's mother will want his remains."

Efrat's eyes drifted away as he nodded. "Yeah, I suppose she would." After a beat, he asked, "What happened back there?"

He wasn't sure what Efrat was referring to—his general murderous rage or the fact that no one, not even Danato, was able to force him off Cori. Ethan was aware of the men clawing at him, trying to breach his grip, but he couldn't feel them. He could feel Levi pushing into his mind, but his presence was barely a whisper of what it usually was. Everything in the room had been muffled—including Cori's kicks and scratches.

Ethan glanced down at his forearms, where he still bore cuts and streaks from her stubby nails. She had dug deep trying to get him off her, but ultimately it was Efrat who was able to remove him. Somehow the power he possessed had snapped him back into reality and thrown him across the room. That much power from Efrat should have killed him, and yet, he was alive. Barely worse for wear beyond the swollen, soon-to-be scarring, spiderweb injury across his back.

"I don't know," Ethan answered honestly. He really didn't know what had happened. Was today part of that magic that he supposedly possessed? Was this what it meant to be a mage? If so, then he really needed to figure out what he was. And perhaps even who he was. Now that he was no longer a father and since he no longer wanted to be a husband or a successor, he needed to discover where he fit in this strange world. Where did he belong? God knows he did not belong here. Not anymore.

Ethan looked over Efrat, sizing him up against the man he used to be. Calm was not the right word for him, but he was definitely content. Joining this ridiculous group had made him feel human again. Apart from today, he would have considered Cori to be the influencing factor in that, but perhaps Ethan had more of a part to play than her. After all, Cori was just another source of frustration for him. And Ethan was… a friend? Yes, he supposed that was what they were now. Friends.

"Why don't you come with me?" Ethan proposed.

Efrat's eyes darted up to Ethan, and his shock turned to amusement. He even sputtered out a laugh. "What?"

Ethan smiled at him and crossed his arms—ignoring the pain in his back. "You heard me. How long has it been since you've seen the outside world?"

Efrat narrowed his eyes. "You know exactly how long it's been."

"Well, then, I'd say it's about time to get reacquainted with it."

"Are you forgetting my handicap?" Efrat waved his hands in the air at him. He flinched at the movement since he was still recovering from his own battle wounds. Danato hadn't held back with either of them.

"We'll choose our travel options carefully." Ethan knew his hands would be an issue, but they were also an advantage.

"Are you serious?" Efrat took a few steps forward as if testing the waters. "Don't you need to get Danato's permission first?"

Ethan's jaw tensed at the mention of his superior's name, and he shook his head. He no longer considered Danato's rules a factor in his life. He no longer considered Danato to be his superior. "I don't need anything from him. Come on, Efrat," Ethan said almost tauntingly. "It's time to go."

Ethan turned and headed into the truck. He stood next to Daniel's coffin and waited. A moment later, Efrat meandered onto the dock and tentatively entered the back of the truck. He looked like a scared animal exploring a new home—excited, but ultimately terrified that it was a trap.

"Hey." Ethan waved over one of the dockworkers and relieved him of his puffy sleeveless vest. The man seemed affronted at losing his winter clothing, but he also didn't want to argue with him. Ethan put the vest on Efrat and zipped it up tight. "These rides are usually pretty cold, and I have no intention of cuddling with you."

The elemental looked at him suspiciously before giving him a cock-eyed grin. "Thanks."

The door slid shut, and the truck rumbled to life. Ethan stayed quiet and tense until the vehicle had cleared the main gate. Once it was in high gear, steadily climbing out of the valley, he sat on a crate and rested his hand on Daniel's coffin.

"Time to go home," he whispered.

35

DANATO WATCHED GYPSY WRITHE and scream on the floor of the infirmary ward just down the back hall from where Leona was resting up. She bounced off bed legs and human legs until she hit Levi's. She looked up at him expectantly, but he only frowned at her. He was glad the staff had put her on the far end of the building where most of her possessed lamentations would not be heard.

"What is wrong with her?"

Levi looked at him guiltily before shrugging. "I think she's succumbing to the dark magic inside her."

"Dark magic? Since when is she magical?"

"She's not," Cleos answered for Levi as he entered the area. "She's the most unmagical being I've ever come into contact with. Besides this negative vortex over here, I mean." Cleos floated his hand in Levi's face as he passed. Levi dodged any potential contact and shifted away from Gypsy. "However, I have sensed something lurking in the background for some time."

"What was lurking?"

"Dark magic," Levi said. "She has it inside her."

"How?" Danato asked.

"That little brat you brought in to execute gave it to her."

"Don't call her a brat!" Levi nearly lunged at Cleos, but his resistance to contact forced him back again. Danato knew that Levi had an abusive history with men, but he wondered if Cleos's abilities made him particularly repugnant to the boy.

"Oh," Cleos crooned, "did I hit a nerve?"

"Someone tell me what the hell is going on!"

"I'll tell you." Cleos volunteered. "While the sorceress was dying, she shed the dark magic that was supposed to be balancing her earth magic. Apparently, the spell wasn't *sticky* enough. Unfortunately, Gypsy came into contact with the magic and took on the full dose in one foul swallow."

"How is that possible—without a ceremony?"

"That's a question I've been asking myself. Perhaps one of the participants can answer it." Cleos turned his accusatory gaze to Levi.

The boy looked between the men, crossing his arms across his chest. "I don't know," he mumbled.

"You don't know, or you don't want us to know?" Cleos asked.

"I don't know! I can't know everything," Levi objected.

"Then perhaps you should figure it out," Cleos snapped.

"Easy, Cleos," Danato grumbled, feeling a little defensive of Levi. "Are you saying Gypsy has had this dark magic inside her since then?" Danato looked at the woman's state of lunacy and shook his head. "How has she been able to function up until now?"

"You're asking the wrong question. Gypsy's condition has made her resistant to human magic. It's not about how she was able to dam the magic. The question is what broke the dam." Cleos frowned down at his underling. "She was a magnificent creature, but something has broken her, and I want to know what—or who?"

"Can you fix her?" Danato asked. "I mean shore up the dam, as you put it? Block the... leak?"

Cleos snarled down at Gypsy. "The magic has permeated her mind."

"Surely you can block out her memory of whatever triggered this, or something."

"He can't," Levi said—perhaps a little smugly. Cleos leered at the boy.

"Why not?" Danato asked. "I thought Cleos was the ultimate black hole of psychic consumption."

Levi snickered. "Yeah, sure, one big bite, but this isn't a bite or a feast. Gypsy has become a vessel."

"Oh yes, we're back to vessels and roads. Both of which were confusing the first time. Please explain again what that means."

"Gypsy isn't holding memories that can be eaten. She is harboring thoughts like..." Levi twisted his lips, considering his words. "She's like a bay. Water flows in and out freely, but she is always full. A vessel for sure, but with recycled content."

"And that content is thoughts?" Danato asked.

"That content is the entirety of all dark magic—human magic. Gypsy is holding the emotions of every living human being on earth inside of her."

"Daniel!" Gypsy screamed. "Get Daniel! Kill them all!" Gypsy leaped from the floor and tangled her hands in Danato's collar. "See me! Hear me!" her voice rasped. "Fight them, Danato! Fight them!" She shook his collar, though it didn't shake him much. "They'll come for you. Do you understand?" Her voice turned to a whimper, and she stroked Danato's cheek. "It's not your fault." Gypsy slapped him, and he finally pushed her off. She laughed maniacally as she backpedaled away from him. She patted her head and sighed. "I'm not quite right, am I?"

"No?" Danato answered.

"Shh." Gypsy raised a finger. "Something's coming." Gypsy looked at Danato and smirked. "Oh, we are all in so much trouble."

"Can we fix this, or not?" Danato asked.

Gypsy made a neck-cutting motion with her hand and snorted when he frowned. "So sensitive. There's no winning team in a war."

"It's possible she can heal herself, but otherwise there is only one thing that can save her."

"What?"

Levi leveled a glare at him. "You know what."

Danato frowned, all at once realizing that Levi was talking about adding earth power to balance the massive amount of dark magic inside of Gypsy. A ceremony that would effectively turn her into a sorceress.

"Unless you would prefer to kill her outright," Levi offered mockingly. Danato was certain the boy's bravado stemmed from the day's stress more than his own will, but since Danato had undergone the same stresses so he considered the boy's timing for pomposity to be unwise.

"You and I need to talk." Levi's eyes widened at the sternness in his *request*. He even shook his head. "Cleos, would you give us some space?"

Cleos glanced between the two of them. He raised an eyebrow and headed for the door. Once he was gone, Danato shifted a little closer to Levi, making the young man tense. Gypsy added herself to the standoff and glared at both of them. "Don't... touch... the rutabaga," she said firmly, scolding them both before retreating to the corner of the room to argue with herself about the value of breathable cotton fabrics.

After a momentary pause to gawk at Gypsy's insanity, Levi said, "If you want to know what happened, you can just ask Cori."

Danato's upper lip twitched as he considered speaking with Cori. He still wasn't ready to see her. He didn't want to hear her voice or even look at her face. He imagined it would be a long time before he could look at her and not see the pale face of his grandson. Regardless of what Cori had to say about the day's events, it was no longer his primary concern.

"I've been remiss in bringing you aboard without some further investigation into your past. Annette warned me to keep you at arm's length—that you had an unhappy history with male figures in your life. But I'm starting to think it's all just a facade to keep *me* from looking too closely at you."

Levi snorted. "You want to see the scars?"

"Zap! Zap! Zap!" Gypsy jumped at the boy with a poking finger, making him recoil only to trip over a bed and flop to the floor on the other side.

"Gypsy!" Danato grabbed her by the shoulders as she continued to point a finger at Levi.

"Zap! Zap! Zap!"

Levi cowered away from her, visibly shaken by her verbal threat.

"Gypsy, stop," Danato commanded.

Gypsy turned to face him, eyes wide. "They cut his wings," she whispered. "He can't fly anymore. You can't fix him." She spoke the words in earnest, and incredibly, her face showed sympathy.

"Okay, Grace," he said soothingly. "I'll be careful with Levi. I won't hurt him anymore."

Gypsy threw her head back and laughed. "You can't hurt him, Danato." Gypsy ran her hands along his biceps somewhat seductively. "Even you're not strong enough to hurt a fae."

Danato glanced back at Levi, ready to dismiss this implication as the words of a crazy woman, but his face had gone pale and his mouth draped open. The eyes staring back at him were no longer those of a nervous young man—but of a terrified boy caught in a lie.

Danato pulled Gypsy aside and pushed her down onto one of the beds. She squeezed his biceps and looked up at him wantonly. "Just one ride? I promise I won't tell."

"Stay," he ordered, and her face fell into a pout. Danato moved to the footrail of the bed that Levi was hiding behind. He leaned his hands on the metal bar and leveled a hard gaze at his newest team member. "I think it's time you told me a little more about yourself, Levi."

Despite his order, Gypsy popped out from behind Danato and braced herself on the foot rail beside him. "Tell him everything," she rasped in a sadistic voice that brought no comfort to the boy.

36

LEVI SQUIRMED ON THE couch as Danato poured himself a strong drink. He glanced back at him, his brow furrowed. "How old are you again?" Levi looked up with the worried gaze of a student being given a pop quiz. "Not that it matters out here." Danato poured a second drink, a quarter of what he had given himself, and handed it to the boy.

Levi examined the drink carefully and then tipped it to his lips. Danato resisted the urge to laugh at his frown of displeasure. He already knew Levi would not be a connoisseur of alcohol the way he and Belus were. Despite his invaluable insights into the world of magic, this place did not suit him. Danato couldn't imagine a future where Levi had a position at the prison. The boy seemed fragile—a perpetually frightened animal, just waiting to flee. Though perhaps that was only what Danato saw because he was the one frightening him.

"Are you sure there isn't anything more we can do for Gypsy?" Danato asked, intentionally starting with a less reflective topic. "I mean besides flooding her with earth power."

Levi shook his head. "I doubt she would survive such a ceremony, anyway. She has virtually no magical essence. Her only saving grace up to this point was her apathy to emotional burdens."

"How did..." Danato clenched his eyes shut and sighed. "I'm sorry, I've forgotten her name."

"Adrianna," Levi supplied. "Addy."

"Yes." Danato took a sip of his drink before continuing. "How did Addy survive so long? As I understood it, she held her dark magic for quite some time."

"She was magically inclined. Her body was used to the flow of magic."

"Still, that is a lot to endure. Is there anything we can do to ease Gypsy's pain?"

Levi coughed on his drink and cleared his throat. "Nothing that would sustain her for long."

Danato noted the rouge on his cheeks, which he was certain was not because of the alcohol. "I was told once that looking at the world through a veil of dark magic allows one to see the truth in all things. Would you agree with that?"

"Dark magic can be used to create masks, but it can also remove them. The mind cannot lie—except to itself."

"I suppose then you'll forgive me for taking some stock in Gypsy's accusation." Levi wouldn't meet his eyes. "It's ridiculous, I know. The fae—what little I know about them—would not lower themselves to associate with humans."

Levi stared at Danato from beneath his brow. "Not by choice."

Danato felt a chill run down his spine, and even the fire in the hearth seemed to falter—dying down to nearly coals. "Levi," he said softly. "Annette wanted me to keep you on here. She felt you had nowhere else to go."

"I don't. Not anymore."

"I've respected her wishes, but if you think I require nothing in return for it, you would be wrong." Levi's eyes lit with fear, and he tensed. Danato narrowed his eyes, dreading the thought of what Levi was thinking at that moment. "I need your honesty, Levi. If you are something more than what you appear to be, then I need to know." Danato leaned forward, placing his drink on the coffee table before settling back in his chair. "What are you?"

Levi set his drink on the coffee table as well. Rather than lean back, he slumped over his knees and stared at his feet. "The fae don't usually take human form. They exist as light more often than as physical beings. That's why it is extremely difficult to capture one. Difficult..." Levi looked up. "But not impossible."

Danato swallowed hard, preparing himself for Levi's next words.

"The iron bars of my cage made it difficult to phase. My captor had also placed spells on it—magical trigger mechanisms that would hurt me if I tried to change forms.

Eventually, he found a buyer for my wings." Levi seemed to curl in on himself, as much ashamed of this history as he was angry.

"Without my wings, I couldn't phase properly." Levi stared into the fire as it bloomed back to life. "I couldn't return to my home. Instead of being a visitor to this world, I became a permanent resident of the earth."

"I'm sorry. I'm sure that was a difficult transition."

Levi looked at Danato squarely. "If it weren't for Annette, I would still be a prisoner. That is the debt I owed her—my appreciation for this life. She was seeking other products from this man. He was a seller of magical antiquities and ingredients. She took one look at me and just... knew." Levi's mouth tipped up as he recalled the memory. "She demanded that the man release me. He wasn't ready to give me up, but—needless to say, she convinced him."

Danato smiled, imagining Annette's indignant response to the man's butchery. People could say what they wanted about the earthen witch's rebellious nature, but she was still a good woman. She was always willing to fight for what she thought was right. Danato only wished he could say the same of himself.

"She freed you?"

"Freed me from my human shackles, but not my earthen ones. I still couldn't leave this realm. At best, I could only pop in and out, like slipping out one door and coming back through another."

"Can you still do that?" Danato asked.

"Yes," Levi answered from the chair across from him. Danato hadn't even seen him disappear before his voice had drawn his eyes. As disconcerting as it was to find out that he could teleport—Danato was more annoyed that Annette had not told him this little detail. It was a very important detail. "She didn't know," Levi said, seemingly answering his thoughts. "I never revealed my abilities to her. She knew I was unaffected by magic because of my origins, and I gratefully assisted in her work to stabilize difficult spells. I also have the ability to calm humans—most humans. I'm not entirely sure why. It's not a skill my people naturally possess, but I imagine it has as much to do with my nature as anything else."

"Why tell me this secret if you never told her?"

Levi frowned. "I wouldn't have told anyone—ever, but Cori and Gypsy figured me out. Chrono-magic is the purview of the fae. I'm not as strong without my wings, but I am able to manipulate the time that surrounds me. That's why I appear to move faster than humans."

"How did they figure you out?"

"Because for several hours before we entered that section, Cori, Gypsy, and Leona were moving faster than your eyes could perceive them. They were moving at my speed."

"That's how we were disrupted."

"Yes."

"How did they achieve that?"

"Gypsy's dark magic cast a spell of intention. She was attempting to give Cori more time. Since that is well beyond her ability, the magic sped them all up instead."

"When did she decide to kill her son?" Danato asked.

Levi's face fell, and he shook his head. "I didn't know she had. We stayed behind to stop all of you from killing each other while Gypsy and Cori left."

"Gypsy went with her?"

"Yes."

Danato was already beginning to form assumptions about how this execution had occurred when the door slammed open. "Danato!" Belus called to him since he was unable to cross the threshold without permission. Surprised by his forcefulness, Danato jumped up to meet him. "He's gone," Belus said even before he reached the door.

"Who?"

"Ethan."

"Gone where?"

"He left the prison." Belus seethed. "And he took Efrat with him."

Danato stood frozen at his front door, staring out into the courtyard as if he might still see remnants of the dust trail left by the vehicle they had stowed away. But of course, there wasn't. Ethan would have left while Danato was preoccupied.

First Duke, then Daniel, his grandchild, and now this. His family was falling apart—one member at a time—and there was nothing he could do to stop it. He backed away from the door, his legs feeling suddenly weak. He wasn't sure if it was simply the stress of the day's conclusion, or if the sorrow demons were latching on.

His knees buckled even as a chair slipped behind him. He barely acknowledged Levi's presence beside him and the chair that had prevented him from crashing to the floor. He pressed trembling hands to his face. "What have I done?" he asked no one in particular.

"Your job," Belus responded coldly from beside him.

Danato looked up at him. "My job was to take that burden. Now she has to live with it. It was supposed to be me—it shouldn't have been anyone, but if it had to be... It should have been me," he whispered."

"She took the burden by choice—as I did. If anyone is to blame, it's me. I trained her too well." Belus rested a hand on his shoulder. "Do you want me to handle Ethan and Efrat?"

"What?" Danato felt suddenly lost in the conversation.

"The collectors."

Danato shook his head. "No, of course not. Ethan is just grief-stricken. He will return."

"He doesn't have permission to leave."

Danato frowned at his second, surprised that even after losing two people he cared for, he didn't have more sympathy for Ethan's desire to flee the situation. It was possible this was his way of dealing with his pain—by throwing himself into work and focusing on the rules. But Danato suspected it was more than grief. Belus was angry. He had just watched Cori perform the same sacrificial act as he had with Olivia. Much like Danato, he was furious that Cori had not allowed them to spare her that indignity.

"It's okay, Belus. Let's just give it a little time. If he's not back in a week or so, we'll make the call."

Belus seemed distressed by this but didn't object. He looked at Levi, who had shifted to stand further back now that Danato was no longer in need of assistance. "Did I interrupt something?"

Danato looked at Levi, who was notably uncomfortable allowing yet another person in on his deepest secrets. "I'll update you in the morning. For now, I think we could all use some sleep."

37

CORI DRAGGED HERSELF OUT of bed and marched down the hall toward the morgue. She needed to see her son. She needed to know it wasn't all a dream. She still couldn't quite believe what she had done. What she had made Gypsy do.

Cori wasn't sure what was wrong with the normally smug woman, but she expected it was something that she could deal with on her own. Cori already had one catastrophic mess to deal with.

She rounded the bend in the hall and ran into a nurse. She tried to usher her back to her room, but Cori all but pushed her off and continued to the morgue. She pushed inside, half expecting to see the baby splayed open for an autopsy. Instead, she found Belus standing next to a metal table, staring at her son's body—eyes glazed and vacant of emotion. She couldn't tell if they looked a little red or if that was her imagination.

"Bel—" Cori coughed, unable to get his name out. Her throat was in a torturous state. Her larynx took the brunt of Ethan's firm grip, and her voice was apparently going to suffer for it.

Belus looked up at her and then immediately looked away. Cori ignored the sting of that rejection. It was no more than she deserved. "What are you doing here? You shouldn't be out of bed."

"I h—" Cori tried to speak again, but she was still limited to what her throat could stand, which wasn't much.

"Don't speak. I already know what you're going to say."

Cori sighed with relief. She knew she could count on Belus to be two steps ahead of her.

"You're going to say that you did this for the good of everyone."

Cori frowned and shook her head.

"When in reality this was just your way of controlling the situation." Belus lifted his eyes to her, revealing a harsh glare. She frowned at him, not understanding his anger. She wasn't to blame for this. The genie was to blame. She was just trying to fix it. "You couldn't allow Danato and me to handle this how we thought best. So, in the end, even when you had concluded we were right, you still had to do it yourself."

Cori blinked at Belus, gleaning only half his statement. She shook her head and dug around in her back pocket. She pulled the medallion out and brought it forward for him to see.

"You're still the same selfish girl you were when you got here."

Cori nearly dropped the badge. She stared at him, appalled that on top of everything, he would strike such a low blow.

"I couldn't be more disappointed in you, Cori." His second blow came much higher than the last, and her heart ached because of it. "We could have handled this together—humanely and medically. Why would you savagely stab your own child?"

"I—" Cori croaked her failing words again. She raised the gold piece a little higher, in case he had not seen it, but his eyes only glanced at it before turning his sharp tongue on her again.

"Ethan left."

She shook her head, not understanding why she should be surprised that Ethan was not waiting by her bedside. She obviously needed to speak with him, but that was not her priority at the moment.

"He took off with Efrat. I'm not sure he's going to be able to forgive you this time," Belus said wistfully. He moved around the table and stopped at the door, but didn't look back at her. "I don't know if any of us will." He left, and Cori stared after him.

His words had summed up to a thousand tiny cuts, but she deserved every one of them. She deserved more than that for what she had done. Which was why she wanted to explain, to make everyone understand why it had to be this way—her way.

Cori looked down at the gold medallion in her hand. The broken top of the weapon she had ordered Gypsy to use to kill her son. It was not especially memorable, but she would have thought Belus of all people would recognize it. Perhaps not, since he had been its victim and not its wielder.

She put aside her concerns about explanations and pleas for forgiveness. In time, they would all see she had made the best possible choice between two horrific options. Until they were willing to listen, she would keep her distance. For now, she needed to be with her son.

She pulled her boy's cold little body into her arms, resting his head on her shoulder as she rocked back and forth with him. His sallow skin was not nearly as frightening as the first time she saw it. He was just sleeping; she told herself. It didn't matter that his heart was not beating, or that he wasn't breathing. He was still her baby boy, and she loved him no matter what.

"We'd better get you out of here," she whispered to him in her sweetest tone. "Can't let those nasty nurses toss you in the fire, can we?" she asked morbidly.

Though he was quiet, Cori searched the room for his pacifier. She found it on the floor underneath the table. As she brought it back up, she noticed something else was missing. Her left ring finger was empty. Someone had taken her wedding ring, and the only person who could remove her empowered rings was Ethan.

She stared at the blank finger for a long time, slowly coming to realize what Belus was telling her. Ethan hadn't just left to commiserate with Efrat. He had left the prison. He was gone.

Her hand shook, and she shushed her son as if he were the one on the verge of tears. "It's okay," she whispered. "It's okay. Daddy will come back. He will. And then we can be a family again. Isn't that right?" She turned to see if her boy was excited about that prospect, but he didn't rouse.

He was still sleeping.

coming soon in The Warden...

There are enemies all around us... and inside of us.

I never thought it would end this way. I never thought I could be ripped from the earth, stripped of the ground beneath my feet, and the breath in my lungs. I can feel it now... deep inside of me, peeking through my eyes, spying with my ears. It wants to come out. It wants to take the reins and, God help me, I'm going to let it. Because if I don't, I'll lose far more than myself.

◆

It was always me who was meant to be the villain. My birthright was destruction, and no matter how much I tried to sheath that blade—I always cut someone in the end. I had hoped to be above all of it—to transcend and be a better person—but it's hard to be a pacifist when people are dying all around you.

◆

I spent my life hating what I had become and despising everyone who had helped make me this way. I had forgotten why I had chosen this path. I had forgotten the war that was brewing beneath the surface. More dangerous than the vampires and the wolves were the faces without fangs. With pen and paper, they have slithered their way up to the top. And now it's my job, my twisted destiny, to stop them... to kill them.

I thought I had lost everything. My family, my job, and my hope for any future happiness. For a fleeting moment, it all came back. But it was there and gone—slipping from my fingers as easily as water through a sieve. I can't let them go again. I can't run away. I can't give up. I'm not sure I understand this new power growing inside of me, but I do know how to use it. And I intend to do just that.

Thank you so much for reading. I hope you enjoyed the ride and if you aren't getting off here, I encourage you to sign up for my newsletter so I can return your generosity with new release updates and special offers.

Sign-Up

You can also find me on Facebook or visit my website. Keep reading!

Website

Facebook

AUTHOR

As a Nebraska native, and a small-town girl at that, I have very little to occupy my time beyond imagining a world outside of my own reality. By the grace of God and the seat of my pants, I have kept my waning attention span on the task of becoming an author.

So here I am, an indie author, peddling my words in cyberspace and enduring my comeuppances with an unwavering determination. I may not be a professional, and I certainly am not perfect, but if you've made it this far, you have to admit, this smartass yokel does spin quite a yarn.

From the self-inflicted sweatshop conditions of my unairconditioned childhood home, to the arthritis reaping positions of a sedentary lifestyle, I bring to you: my sarcasm, my oddity, and my heart. Take it with a grain of salt or a teaspoon of sugar, but take it for what it is: a story born of the mind, translated to paper, and gifted to you.

I thank you for your readership and even more for your support. Please recommend this book to your friends and family via any social media that you use. Word of mouth is still the best advertising and is greatly appreciated.

Most importantly, keep reading. I'll keep writing.